AXEL'S GRIND

(SAVAGE HELL MC BOOK 5)

K.L. RAMSEY

Axel's Grind (Savage Hell MC Book 5)

Copyright © 2022 by K.L. Ramsey

Cover Design: Michelle Sewell at RLS Images Graphics & Design

Imprint:Independently published

First Print Edition: January 2022

All rights reserved.

No part of this book may be reproduced, scanned, or distributed in any printed or electronic form without permission. Please do not participate in or encourage piracy of copyrighted materials in violation of the author's rights. Thank you for respecting the hard work of this author.

This is a work of fiction. Names, characters, places, and incidents either are the product of the author's imagination or are used fictitiously, and any resemblance to locales, events, business establishments, or actual persons—living or dead—is entirely coincidental.

AXEL

Axel walked into his newly empty apartment and dropped his bike's keys on the kitchen counter. His bitch of an ex-girlfriend was finally gone, and he was happy to be rid of her. His best friend, Hart, was right—Ginger was nothing but trouble and he was better off without her.

They had been together for almost a year and when he broke it off with Ginger, she packed up her shit and took off with all of his furniture, claiming that he owed her for the last year of her life. She said that he was a waste of her fucking time, and he had to admit, he felt the same way about her. If losing his furniture was the only way to get her out of his life, it was worth it. Besides, he could just go and buy some new furniture, but that bitch was gone forever.

A soft knock at the door made him groan out loud. The last thing he wanted or needed was to deal with someone dropping by his now empty apartment—especially his blissfully, newly married business partner who had just gotten back from his extended honeymoon. He was looking forward to having Hart around again, to help pick up with some of the cases that were quickly piling up on his desk at work, but he was hoping that all could wait until morning.

He pulled the door open and growled, "What," at the pretty little brunette who stood on the other side of it.

"Um, I'm sorry to bother you at your home," she squeaked. She looked terrified—hell, terrified didn't even begin to cover the horrific way that she looked at him.

"I'm sorry, I thought that you might be someone else," he admitted. "Are you all right?" he asked. The dark-haired beauty looked around the hallway as if checking to make sure that no one was watching them.

"No," she leaned into whisper. "I think I'm being followed, and I need your help. Are you Axel Lopez?" she asked. "The one with the detective agency," she quickly added.

"I am," he said. "You are?"

She looked around nervously again and nodded as if satisfied that she wasn't followed to his place. "My name is Melody Valentine." Her name was so pretty that it almost sounded fake. He wasn't sure whether to shake her outstretched hand or to laugh at the alias she used. He went with option number one, just in case her name wasn't fake.

He slid his hand into her own, "Nice to meet you, Melody," he said. "How about you come in and we can chat about what my agency can do for you." She quickly took him up on his offer, stepped into his apartment, and looked around as he shut the front door.

"You a minimalist?" she asked.

He chuckled, "No," he admitted. "My ex took all of the furniture when she took off."

"Oh, I'm sorry," Melody breathed.

"Don't be. She did me a favor in taking off, so I guess I got a pretty good deal," he said.

"Things didn't end well?" Melody asked. She was asking a lot of personal questions for a woman who needed his help.

"I'm sorry, why did you say that you've come here, Melody? What exactly do you need my help with?" he asked.

"Well, I might not have been one hundred percent truthful with you, Axel," she said. She suddenly didn't seem as nervous as she had been out on his doorstep.

"Your name is fake, right?" he asked.

"No," she said, "that part was the truth. But I'm not really in trouble. I'm afraid that you might be though."

"I might be in trouble?" he asked. The idea was laughable. No one was coming after him—he wasn't the type of guy who had a lot of enemies, and he liked it that way. "How so?" he asked. He had a feeling that this was going to be good. He walked over to his refrigerator and pulled out two cold beers, holding one up to Melody, offering it to her.

She shook her head, "Can't," she breathed. "I'm on duty." Fuck—she was a cop.

"So, not a damsel in distress," he said. "You're a cop, aren't you Melody?" he asked. He could tell that he had guessed correctly and when she pulled her badge from her side buckle, which she had kept hidden under her jacket, he wanted to groan out loud. What the fuck had just happened?

"You know that I invited you into my home under false pretenses, right?" he asked. "If you're here to serve me or to question me about one of my clients, I think that it's best that you leave now." Axel leaned back against the kitchen counter, taking a swig of his beer, waiting her out.

She smiled and put her badge back. "I'm not here about one of your clients, and I don't serve people—that's grunt work and I'm no grunt. I'm here to ask you a few questions about a homicide case that I'm working on—one that I think might interest you."

"A homicide case?" he asked. "I haven't worn a badge in a damn long time, and I have no plans on going back to that life, Melody. Now, if you will excuse me, I have an air mattress to blow up and a few hours of sleep to get before I have to start my workday." He held out his hand in the direction of the front door, hoping that she'd pick up on his not-so-subtle hints that he wanted her to leave.

"I get it, Axel. I know about your time on the force, and I also know why you left." No one knew the real reason that he left, but he was too tired to call her on her bullshit. He just couldn't take the grind anymore. He hated the paperwork that went with each incidence that seemed to occur daily. Hell, it wasn't even worth handing out a ticket anymore because of the grunt work that followed. When

Hart asked him to start a detective agency with him, he jumped at the chance. Sure, they still had the paperwork and everything that went with owning their own business, but it was theirs and they did things on their terms. If they didn't want to take a case, they turned it down. It was just that simple.

"You don't know me," he spat as she turned to leave.

"Sure, Axel," she said, handing him her business card on the way out. "Give me a call when you're ready to talk about my case. It involves someone that I think you know—well, intimately," she said. "Ginger Basset was found dead Tuesday morning."

"Fuck," he breathed. That was the day that she packed up all of her shit and told him that she'd be back for her stuff when she could line up the moving truck and some help. It was the last time that he saw her. "Am I a suspect?" he asked. He knew the drill—everyone was a suspect until they could provide an alibi. He thought hard about where he was every day for the past week and most of his time would be considered unaccountable. He was on stakeouts by himself since Hart was out of town on his honeymoon.

"You know how this works, Axel," she said. "Everyone's a suspect—especially the people closest to her. How about you come down to the station and help me cross your name off of my list of suspects and then, you can come back here and blow up your air mattress?" she taunted. He had a feeling that she wasn't really asking him if he wanted to join her; more like telling him how things were going to go down.

"You're not asking me to come down to the station with you, are you, Melody?" he asked.

"No, not really. My partner and I will be waiting just outside your front door. Take a few minutes and then feel free to join us." He laughed at her choice of words. Nothing about this had anything to do with him, "Feeling free."

"Will I need a lawyer?" he asked.

"Well, that is completely up to you," she said.

"Am I being arrested?" he asked.

"No," Melody said. "Not if you agree to come down to the station with us willingly. We just want to ask you a few questions, Axel," she insisted, her smile easy. He remembered this routine. He had fed the same lines to so many guys that he ended up helping to put behind bars. He wondered if Melody was hoping to do the same with him.

"Give me two minutes, and I'll be out," he said. He hated that this was going to happen, but what choice did he have—none. She nodded and stepped out into the hallway, pulling his front door shut behind her. He was going to be smart about all of this and do things by the book. He knew that calling in a lawyer might make him look guilty as hell, but there was no way that he'd walk into that station without one.

He called Savage's number and breathed a sigh of relief when his club's Prez answered on the second ring. "Savage," he said into the other end of the phone.

"It's Axel. Sorry to bother you, man, but I think I could use some help."

"Name it," Savage said. He knew that the guy meant it too. He'd do just about anything to help out one of his own, that was the way that their MC worked.

"I need a lawyer," he said. "Any of the guys wear that hat during the day?" he asked. Their little motley crew was made up of guys from all walks of life—most of them were ex-military. He knew that Savage had a ton of connections and would be his best bet for showing up at the station with legal representation.

"Yeah—we have a guy in Savage Hell who can help you out," Savage said. "His name's Razor and he's a good guy. I've known him for about ten years now. He'll be able to help you out."

"Great," Axel said. "Have him meet me downtown at the station as soon as possible. I'll stall until he gets there. I think I'm being questioned for murder."

"Shit," Savage growled into the phone. "Who's?" he asked.

"My ex's," Axel said. "Thanks for this man—I owe you."

"Not a problem," Savage said. "Just try to keep your mouth shut until Razor gets there. I'll tell him to hurry up."

"Will do, man," Axel agreed. The knock at his front door told him that his time was up. "Got to go, Savage. Thanks," he said and ended the call. Axel just hoped like hell that he could find a way to stall because if not, he had a feeling that his time would really be up. Melody Valentine was out for blood, and he had a feeling that his would work just fine for her.

MELODY

MELODY SAT ACROSS FROM THE MAN SHE BELIEVED TO BE HER key suspect and stared him down—not that her tactics would work on someone like Axel Lopez. The guy was practically a legend in the station and bringing him in on the Basset murder might be the final nail in her career's coffin.

Her captain told her not to even question the guy about his ex ending up dead behind her new apartment building. She had tried to convince her boss that Axel was a prime suspect and should be questioned about Ginger Basset's murder, but he was adamant to leave Axel out of this mess. That was just something that she couldn't do, not when her gut was screaming at her that he not only did it, but he had the means and know-how to cover up her murder or make it look like someone else did it.

In her opinion, it was a crime of passion—she left him,

and he got pissed off and killed her. If Axel couldn't have her, no one could, and now, all she had to do was prove it. That might be the part that proved damn near impossible since she got word that her boss was on his way back down to the station and he wasn't at all happy about the fact that she went against his orders and brought Lopez in for questioning.

"How about we save ourselves some time and you just tell me what happened. I'm sure that the DA would be happy to cut a deal for our hometown hero," she lied. She had no clue as to how the DA would approach a case like this one, especially if it did come down to Axel Lopez being guilty.

"You and I both know that's not how this thing works. I won't confess to a crime that I didn't commit, and I've already told you that I want to wait for my lawyer to get here. I'm sure that we can get to the bottom of this after he arrives," Axel offered.

Melody sat down across from him and smiled. "You and I both know that's not how this thing works," she said, giving him back his words. "Your lawyer shows up here and finds a way to avoid answering any of my questions and then he gets you out of here. We'll end up going around and around in circles and that poor woman's death will go unsolved. Why not help me out here, Axel?" she asked. "You two were close, right. I mean you did live together until recently. What happened? Why did she take off with all of your furniture? I bet that pissed you off," she taunted. He crossed his arms over his massive chest and smirked across the table at her.

Melody could tell that he wasn't going to budge on the whole, "I want to wait for my lawyer," bit, and she'd have no choice but to play by the rules once he showed up to represent Axel.

"You know, besides the fact that you're accusing me of being a murderer, I like you, Melody," he said. "You have spunk and persistence—two qualities that I admire in a police detective."

"Does that mean that you'll answer my questions?" she asked.

"No," he breathed. "But I'll give you credit for trying."

She wanted to tell him that he could shove his credit right up his ass, but she didn't get the chance to. The heavy metal door swung open and the biggest man she had ever seen in her life stood in the doorway, wearing a three-piece suit that looked as if it was tailor-made for him. He walked over to Axel and handed him his business card; his smile was mean.

"I'm your lawyer, Razor," he said, his deep baritone booming through the office. "Savage sent me."

"Good to meet you, Razor," Axel said, shaking the big guy's hand. "Thanks for coming in on such short notice."

"Not a problem. I hear that you've been asked to come in for questioning," Razor said, looking between where Axel and Melody sat. "Might I ask what for?" he directed his question at Melody.

"His girlfriend's murder," she said.

"Ex-girlfriend," Axel corrected.

"How about you let me give the answers here, man.

That's why Savage called me in," Razor said. Axel waved his hand as if telling him to be his guest and Melody almost wanted to giggle at the whole scene. The two big, bad bikers were practically comparing dick sizes while she looked on.

"Have at it," Axel agreed.

"I'd like to talk to my client alone if you don't mind. Then, you and I can talk about getting him out of here and maybe we can grab some dinner," he said.

"Smooth," she grumbled. Melody didn't date lawyers—or cops for that matter, no matter how sexy they were or how hot they made her. "Having dinner with you would be a conflict of interest, Mr. Razor," Melody said.

"It's just Razor," he insisted. "And, how so?"

"Well, you are representing a man who I believe killed the woman whose case I'm working. That would make us having dinner tonight, or any night for that matter, a really bad idea. I appreciate the offer though," she lied. "I'll give you and your client ten minutes to talk." She stood and headed for the door, knowing that they were both watching her leave the room. That was just fine with her—she could put on a show and have them forgetting what they should or shouldn't say in just seconds. It was a gift, really, and Melody had no issues with using her looks to get what she wanted. And right now, she wanted an open and shut case to add to her file. She needed a win and she'd take it just about any way that she had to.

Melody walked right into her boss on her way out the

door and he quickly ushered her into the observation room. "What the fuck is going on here, Valentine?" he asked.

"I think that Lopez is connected to the Basset murder. He openly admitted that he was involved with her up until a few days ago and that she took all of his furniture when she left him. I think it was a crime of passion. Maybe he decided that he couldn't live without her once she was gone, and he killed her."

"Or maybe, they were just two people who used to date, things ended, and she left him," her Sargent insisted. "Because sometimes, that happens. You and I know that better than anyone, Melody"

"She took all of his furniture," she said. "That has to piss a person off—having all of their belongings taken right out from under them."

"Maybe he's the type of guy who doesn't put much stock in personal belongings. Maybe he was fine with losing his shit if it meant that she was out of his life," her Sargent said.

"Or maybe he killed her to remove her from his life permanently." Melody knew that going back and forth like this could last all day with her boss. He loved to play devil's advocate with her, especially when he thought she was wrong—and he definitely believed that she was wrong about Lopez.

"Does he have an alibi?" her boss asked.

"He sure does," his lawyer said, stepping into the observation room and shutting the door behind himself. "My client was at his club when the murder allegedly occurred. He has an air-tight alibi. So, if you wouldn't mind, we'd like to be on our way."

"We have a few more questions," Melody insisted.

Her boss shot her a look and huffed out his breath. "No, we don't," he said. "Will his alibi hold up in court? Will others from his MC collaborate his being there that night?" he asked.

"Yes," Razor said. "He has many witnesses willing to testify that Axel was at Savage Hell most of the night. His alibi will hold up in court."

"Shit," her boss grumbled. "Release him," he said, turning back to face Melody. "And next time, follow my fucking orders," he breathed.

"Yes, Sir," Melody said. She hated being wrong and for some reason, she had a feeling that she just wasn't when it came to Axel Lopez. He was bad news and just because her boss refused to see it, didn't make it any less true. One way or another, she planned on proving that she was right, even if it meant going against orders again and putting her job on the line. The one thing Melody hated being was wrong.

AXEL

Axel walked out of the police station and breathed in the crisp night air. "I didn't think you'd be able to get me out of there tonight, Razor," he admitted. "Detective Valentine seemed determined to link me to my ex's murder. Thank you." He held out his hand to Razor and the big guy grabbed it into his own and shook it.

"That's what brothers are for, Axel," he insisted. "Besides, I owed Savage one. Hell, if I'm being honest, I owe him a few, but who's counting. When that guy calls me, I just help him, no questions asked."

"So, you won't be asking me if I murdered my ex-girlfriend then?" Axel asked.

"Nope," Razor said. "I don't care one way or the other. My job is to keep you out of prison, period. I plan on doing my job, Axel, and I'm damn good at it too."

"I appreciate that, man. For the record, I didn't kill her. In fact, I didn't even know that she was dead until Detective Valentine told me, just before she asked me to come down to the station with her," Axel said.

"Any idea who'd want her dead?" Razor asked.

"No clue. Ginger was a pain in the ass, but I can't think of anyone who'd want her dead. I'd like the chance to find out though. I owe her at least that much. We just spent the better part of a year together," Axel admitted. He never loved Ginger, and that was the major reason why he'd told her that he just couldn't be with her anymore. She didn't take it very well, demanding that she was his Ol'lady and that his club would be hearing about him just letting her go the way he was. She even threatened to go into Savage Hell to find herself another biker, but Axel knew that none of his brothers would touch her without his permission. She was his and that meant that the guys wouldn't go near Ginger without asking him first. It was their code and the guys of the Royal Bastards lived and died by their codes.

"You need to stay the fuck away from this mess, Axel," Razor ordered. "I got you out of there this time, but you go and do something stupid, I might not be so lucky next time. What I can promise you is that Detective Valentine doesn't seem like the kind of chick to just back down."

"No, she doesn't," Axel agreed.

"I saw what you did in there—she believes that you did it. Lucky for us, her boss doesn't share her opinion and he's the reason why you're standing here. I told them about you being at Savage Hell on the night she was murdered. Will the guys back you up? Did anyone see you there?"

"Savage was there that night and his husband, Bowie, was the bartender. I was there to drown my sorrows, but after two beers I gave up. I realized I wasn't as torn up about her leaving me as I originally thought I was. So, I hung out with a few of the guys playing pool—Ryder and Cillian were in that group, and then I headed back home after a few games."

"I'll warn them that they will probably have a little visit from the sexy detective. I have to admit, I'm not upset about the possibility of her showing up at the club. I didn't mind looking at her," Razor admitted.

"Yeah, I picked up on that," Axel said. "How about you stay away from her, and I'll promise not to snoop around my ex's case. I have a feeling that if you start fucking the detective on the case, I'll end up having to find another lawyer."

Razor chuckled and slapped his shoulder, practically sending him flying a few feet forward. "I like you, Axel," he said. That was good because Axel had a feeling that having Razor for an enemy would be a bad thing.

"Thanks," Axel breathed, rubbing his shoulder. "You're great too, man." He felt like he was making a declaration, and, in some cultures, they'd be engaged or something.

"Okay, enough of this mushy shit. How about I let you buy me a beer at Savage Hell and then, I'll run you home?" Razor asked.

"Thanks, man," Axel said. "Detective Valentine insisted that I ride down here with her and her officer."

"Figured, and it's no problem," Razor assured. "You ready?"

"Absolutely," Axel agreed. The last thing he wanted was to stick around the parking lot at the police station. He had had enough of this God-awful day and was ready to have a few beers and then hit the air mattress, which he still had to blow up.

Tomorrow, he was going to have to get a few essentials, including a bed and couch. He didn't need all of the comforts of home, but his back wouldn't last sleeping on an air mattress and sitting on the floor to watch television wasn't his idea of a good time.

Then, he was going to have to fill in his business partner, Hart, about what had just gone down. He had a feeling that his partner wasn't going to like the fact that he had gotten mixed up in a murder rap, but there wasn't anything he could do about this mess. Hart hated Ginger and made no efforts to hide his feelings about her. Axel was pretty sure that his partner wouldn't be upset to hear the news that she was dead, but he'd hate that Axel and their detective agency was going to have to deal with a possible scandal. That was the very last thing that their new little company needed. They were just getting started and any kind of bad publicity would possibly put a black mark on their good name. Yeah—Hart was probably going to give him an earful, but he'd worry about all that in the morning. Right now, beer and his brothers were on his radar, and that sounded like a perfect way to end his night.

By the time he and Razor got to the bar, the guys were winding down from a night of celebrating a few new patched members. Savage saw them as soon as they walked into Savage Hell and nodded for them to join him at the bar. Axel wasn't going to argue with his club's Prez. He needed a beer A.S.A.P.

"I take it things went well since you're standing in my bar," Savage said.

"They did," Razor agreed. Axel wasn't sure if he'd call what happened ending well, but Savage was right—at least he was there. Savage's husband, Bowie, poured them both a beer and by the time he downed the first one, Axel felt a bit more relaxed.

"Now, want to tell me what's going on?" Savage asked as if he was waiting for Axel to get his beer down before prying.

"You remember my girlfriend, Ginger?" Axel asked.

"Ex-girlfriend," Razor corrected. "You need to change your terminology."

"Right, ex-girlfriend. We broke up and she took off with all of our stuff. I was fine with that because she was gone, you know? I'd love to say that I was torn up about her taking off, but I wasn't. I was relieved."

"Shit," Razor grumbled, nodding to Bowie for another round. "That's not something that you ever say out loud again either. You were nursing a broken heart if anyone asks you—got it?"

"Yeah, yeah," Axel said. "I know the routine, man. You do know that I used to be a cop, right?"

"From the limited research that I was able to do on my way down to the station tonight, yes. But that fact won't save you when push comes to shove. Melody Valentine won't give a fuck who you used to be as she comes after you for your ex's murder. And believe me, she's coming. I saw the determination in her eyes."

"Who is Melody Valentine?" Savage asked.

"I was getting to that," Axel said. "Just minutes after I got home tonight from work, this woman showed up on my doorstep claiming to need help. God, she looked so afraid, I just let her into my place. I wanted to help her, but I knew that something was up the second she started asking me questions. She asked too many of them and when I called her on it, she finally told me who she was."

"Entrapment," Razor growled.

"Yeah—I told her so, but she didn't give a fuck. She insisted that I go down to the station with her and honestly, she gave me no other option. So, I went with her and the cop who was riding with her, but before I did, I called Savage to get his help."

"That's when you called me, right?" Razor asked.

Savage grunted and nodded. "I figured he needed a lawyer who'd be able to get his ass out of there, and that person is you," Savage said. "It's why the club keeps you on retainer."

"You keep a lawyer on retainer?" Axel asked.

"Yep," Savage said. "My guys seem to find trouble and I like to have a lawyer who is tough as nails and can handle any shit they get into—that's you." Axel looked Razor over, wondering what was so special about him. He was a big guy who seemed to demand control and respect as soon as he walked into the room, but there was something more.

"You're ex-military," Axel said. Most of the guys in Savage Hell were either ex-military or in some form of law enforcement. Hell, they even had a few FBI agents in their motley crew. It kept things interesting and if Savage kept the big guy around to represent them all when they found trouble, he had to have some understanding of who they were as men.

"I am," Razor said. "Army Ranger," he said. "When I got out, I finished college and went to law school. I wasn't really sure what I wanted to do with my life, but I finally figured it out. All I knew was that I wanted to help people—people like me. I found that here in Savage Hell. I love that our little club is a part of the Royal Bastards and that I can help not only our crew, but brothers all over the world. When Savage calls, I go where he tells me to go. That's just the way things work."

"Well, I appreciate you coming down to rescue my ass tonight," Axel said.

"You know, the question remains—who killed your ex?" Bowie asked from behind the bar.

Axel shrugged, "Don't know," he said. "But I'd like to find out, even though Razor's against me doing some snooping around."

"Because you'll end up getting your ass in even more trouble and I don't have time for that shit," Razor grumbled.

"I think that I can help do a little recon," Savage said. "Well, Bowie and me. My husband has a way of finding things out about people they don't want to be found. Want to do a little digging, babe?" Savage asked Bowie.

"You know it," Bowie agreed, giving his husband a coy wink. "I'll start first thing in the morning."

"Thanks, man," Axel said. "I'd really like to help though. I mean, I do own part of a detective agency."

"Who owns the other part of it?" Razor asked.

"Another member. His name is Hart," Savage said. "Why?"

"How about letting your partner take lead on this investigation?" Razor asked. "That way you can be a part of it all and still not technically involved. It will just sit better with the cops if you don't start looking around."

"Fine," Axel grumbled. "I'll talk to Hart about all of this in the morning. He just got back from his honeymoon, and I don't want to bother him and his woman this late at night. You mind giving me a ride home?" Axel asked Razor.

"Not at all," he said. "We'll be in touch in the morning," Razor told Savage.

"Thanks for everything, man," Savage said.

"Don't mention it," Razor said. "Let's go, Axel," he ordered.

MELODY

Melody sat in her car just outside of Axel's apartment, waiting for him to get home. "Where the fuck is he?" she grumbled to herself. Usually, for a steak out, she'd have a partner along, but she was going rogue for this mission, and asking any one of her fellow officers to join her might end up with them both losing their jobs. She couldn't risk that.

After she pushed through Lopez's paperwork, she was called into her captain's office so that he could scream at her some more. He was pissed that she went against orders and brought Lopez in. That was fair since she had always been a rule-breaker and this latest mishap seemed to really rub her boss the wrong way.

When she first got the case, she researched Ginger Basset and Axel Lopez's name popped up. They had been together for about a year, until recently, when Ginger packed up all of her stuff and left. From the look of his empty apartment, she packed up some of his stuff too, and that had to infuriate a man like Axel. She essentially stole his shit and that would meet with some form of punishment in his world—possibly even death. Melody just needed the proof.

She sat through her boss's lecture and by the time he finished, the trail had run cold for her to follow Axel. Melody had only one choice and it was probably going to get her fired unless she was right. She drove across town and parked in the back of the parking lot at Axel's apartment. His truck was still parked in the same spot it was in earlier; his motorcycle parked next to it. Melody wondered if he was home but walking up to his front door and knocking on it wasn't an option. So, she sat and waited for any sign of life coming from his place.

It was almost midnight when a car she recognized pulled into the parking lot. It was his lawyer's car—what was his name? Oh yeah, Razor. He pulled up in front of Axel's building and looked straight back to where she sat, even pointing her out to Axel.

"Shit," she grumbled, sinking into her car seat, praying that it would swallow her up whole. Razor looked like he was asking Axel something, to which he shook his head and got out of Razor's SUV. Melody watched as the lawyer sped out of the parking lot, giving her one last look back. Axel, on the other hand, didn't bother looking back at her as he walked into his apartment building. She wasn't sure if she should stay or take off for the night, since she had been made.

Honestly, she had nothing and no one to go home to, so she decided to stick around for a bit to see if anything happened. She watched as his apartment lights went on and then, just moments later, they went off again. Axel seemed to be going to bed and honestly, that sounded like a damn good idea. It felt like ages since she had gotten a good night's sleep.

Melody closed her eyes for just a few seconds, or so she thought. She woke up to someone beating on her window as if they wanted to break it in. She peeked her eyes open only to be blinded by the bright sunlight. What the hell had happened? She closed her eyes for just a split second and now, she had a very angry biker standing next to her car, beating on her window.

She quickly turned on her car to lower her window and yawned, covering her mouth with her hand. "What can I do for you Mr. Lopez?" she asked.

"You can tell me what the hell you're doing in front of my apartment building still," he said.

"Well, I was making sure that whoever took out your ex wasn't going to show up here for you next," she lied. That was a good cover though. Maybe it would work with her boss too.

"Not buying it," he insisted. Shit—that was what she was afraid of.

"I don't care if you buy it or not, Lopez," she lied again. If he went to her boss, she could be fired, and she really needed her job. But more than that, she liked her job.

"You're here to keep an eye on me because you think that I killed her," he said.

"Did you?" she asked.

"I've already told you that I didn't. That was the only free question that I'll answer without my lawyer present, Detective. If you're going to haul me back down to the station, let me know now, so I can give Razor a call to have him meet me." The last thing that she planned on doing was hauling him back down to the station. Her boss would have her ass if she did that again against his orders.

"I'm not going to haul you in, Axel," she assured. "I'm just searching for answers, and I think that you might be the answer I'm searching for."

"I'm sure that I'm not the guy to help you out with that," he insisted. "Answers are hard to come by and usually lead to more questions. It's a dangerous rabbit hole to go down," he insisted.

"How about you let me decide if I want to go down the dangerous rabbit hole?" she asked. "You want to end this little game and just answer a few questions for me?"

"No," he said.

"Did your lawyer tell you to say no to me?" she asked.

"Yes," he admitted. "And I agree with him. Talking to you isn't a good idea," he admitted. "I just want to know who killed Ginger."

"Smooth," she said. "Because it wasn't you, right?"

"Correct," he agreed. He was a really good liar. He looked her dead in the eye before telling her that he wasn't responsible for his ex-girlfriend's death, and that just couldn't be the truth.

"So, asking you out to breakfast would be a no from you then?" she asked. He looked a bit indecisive, and she wondered if she was starting to wear down his defenses.

"Just breakfast, no questions?" he asked.

"Do you plan on asking me questions?" she asked. The look on his face told her that he was planning on asking her a bunch of questions. "How about for every question you ask me, I get to ask you one in return?" she asked. "You can even call this one off the books," she said. "Nothing you say can be used against you." He looked like he wanted to call bullshit, but instead, he nodded his agreement. Melody wasn't sure how or why he'd agreed to have breakfast with her, but she wasn't about to look gift horse in the mouth.

"You want to ride with me?" she asked.

"No," he said. "I'll take my truck. I have to head into the office after our breakfast to meet with a new client."

"Fair enough," she said. "I'll meet you then. How about that little diner on the corner of Fifth and Cornwall?" she asked.

"I love that place," he agreed. "See you there." She nodded and turned on her engine as he walked over to her truck. Melody wasn't sure if this little breakfast was a good or bad thing, but she was about to find out.

Axel's Grind

Melody walked into the diner, half expecting to not find Axel there—but he was. She found him sitting in the corner booth and she once again wondered to herself if this was a good idea. If her boss found out that she was secretly meeting with Axel Lopez, he'd have her badge. This time, there would be no sweet-talking him out of it either since Melody wasn't sleeping with him anymore. Yeah—that was a colossally bad idea.

When she started up with her captain, he wasn't her boss. She was in an entirely different precinct, and he wasn't her superior. Joel was a nice guy and when he asked her out, she told him, yes, not thinking about the consequences. Why would she, really? When they just started out, she never saw their career paths crossing as they had. As soon as they found out that not only would they be working together, but that he'd be her boss, she broke it off. They had only been dating for four months, but it still hurt like a bitch to have to let him go. She found a way to move on though, and so did he. They both learned to rely on their friendship to help cure all of the uncomfortable bumps along the way, but they were managing.

Maybe that's why she felt so comfortable in pushing him a bit. She always took things to the next level, knowing that Joel would never fire her for a decision that she had to make while in the field. But lately, she could feel that she was pushing him too far—asking for too much, and sooner or later, her grace with him would be lost. She'd ask for too much, or push him too far, and Joel would have no choice but to can her.

She walked up to the corner booth where Axel sat and slipped in across from him. "Thank you for agreeing to meet with me," she said.

"I only agreed because I'm hoping to put a stop to your ridiculous notion that I killed my ex. I would never do something like that, but you don't know me, so I won't put that on you. I'd really like to figure out who did it though. I might not have ended things with Ginger on a positive note, but I'd never wish her dead. I don't know of many people who would," he said. She had to hand it to him, she almost believed him—almost.

The waitress came to their booth and took their breakfast orders, promising to bring them coffee, and collecting their menus on her way back behind the counter. "So, we're going to play twenty questions, then?" he asked. She had so many questions, Melody was sure that twenty wouldn't cover them all.

"Sure," she agreed.

"You can go first, Detective," he insisted. "You look about ready to explode, you're so anxious to get your answers."

"Were you really at a bar during the time of the murder?" she asked. He could lie to her, but she was usually pretty good at detecting a lie. She just hoped that her radar wasn't off just because she found Axel Lopez so damn sexy. Melody always did love a bad boy, and she was pretty sure that even if he wasn't a stone-cold killer, he'd fit the bill.

"Yes," he said. "I'd be happy to give you the names of the guys I was hanging out with that night," he said.

"So that they can lie for you?" she asked.

"Is that your second question?" Axel asked. "Because if it is, I'm going to start keeping count for when it's my turn. Tit for tat, Detective."

"Sure, it can be my second question," she griped.

He chuckled, "My buddies are a lot of things—some even ex-cons, but they aren't liars. They would have my back, no questions asked, but they wouldn't lie to do it."

"What's the name of the bar that you were hanging out at?" she asked. Axel held up a third finger and she rolled her eyes at him and nodded.

"Savage Hell," he said. "It's where my club meets and my buddy, Savage owns it."

"Well, that's convenient," she grumbled. "So, I'm assuming this Savage guy will vouch for you then?" she asked. He added another finger, keeping count of her questions, and she sighed.

"Yes," he said. "Savage was there that night, and so was his husband, Bowie. I really don't mind getting you a list of names together, Detective."

"I wish you'd call me Melody," she breathed. Having him call her "Detective" reminded her that she wasn't on the job and that questioning him was a huge mistake, even if she was getting answers. The only problem was, they weren't the answers that she was hoping for. The longer that she sat there, the more she was beginning to believe that he was telling the truth and that chapped her ass.

"Fine, Melody," he said. The way that he whispered her name felt personal, almost like a caress and she wrapped her arms around her body, trying to ward off a shiver.

"Are you cold?" he asked. Axel didn't wait for her answer, standing to remove his leather jacket and wrap it around her shoulders. It smelled like him with a hint of cigar smoke, and she smiled, remembering how her grandfather used to smoke cigars when she was just a kid.

"Thank you," she said.

"Not a problem," Axel said.

"Do you smoke cigars?" she asked.

"That's five questions and yes," he admitted. "Well, occasionally. My buddy's Ol'lady just had his kid, and we celebrated the other night. Sorry if the jacket smells like smoke," he said. "Want me to take it back?"

"No," she quickly said. "I don't mind it. In fact, I kind of like the smell. It reminds me of my grandpa. He used to smoke cigars around me, and it used to make my mother so mad. I miss him."

"I'm sorry," Axel breathed. "How long ago did he pass?" he asked.

She held up her finger and smiled at him. "That's question number one," she said.

"Actually," he said. "It's question number four," he admitted. She thought back over their conversation, trying to figure out what the hell he was talking about. Axel chuckled, "I asked you if your second question was your second question. Then, I asked if you were cold and when you asked about the cigar smoke, I asked if you wanted me to take my jacket back. Last, I asked when your grandpa passed, which you still haven't answered."

"Shit," she grumbled, "you might be better at this game than I am. My grandpa passed when I was just a teenager. It was tough because my mother and I lived with him and well, his house wasn't the same without him in it."

"I get that," Axel admitted. "My parents passed when I was an older teen and I ended up taking care of my little brother. I was eighteen, alone and taking care of a ten-year-old little boy. I was way out of my comfort zone."

"I bet," she whispered. "That had to be hard. What happened to your parents?"

"Car wreck," he said. Axel lowered the hand that had been keeping score back to the table and sat back in the booth. She could tell from his body language that he might be relaxing a bit, and that would mean that he'd let his guard down at some point. She hoped that was the case because she still wasn't sure if he was telling her the truth or not.

"I'm sorry," she said.

"Drunk driver hit them head-on," he said. "Killed them both instantly."

Her next question might piss him off, but now she was curious. "Ginger's blood alcohol levels came back in her toxicology report this morning. She was legally drunk. Was alcohol an issue for her?" she asked.

He sighed, "Yes," Axel said. "She was a heavy drinker. It's one of the things that I hated most about our relationship. Ginger would go and get rip-roaring drunk and then make a fool of herself at Savage Hell. She hit on most of my buddies, and they all laughed it off, but it still hurt, you know."

"I'm sure that it did," Melody agreed. "She made you angry."

"What—no," he insisted. "She embarrassed me, but she never made me angry—at least not angry enough to kill her. That's what you were getting at, right?" he asked.

Melody sat forward and smiled. "Caught me," she teased.

Axel rolled his eyes. "You know, you never told me how she died. I'm guessing that was to trap me if I figured it out, but I can't for the life of me, I can't imagine anyone wanting to kill Ginger. Yeah, she was a drunk and kind of a pain in the ass, but that doesn't warrant murder."

"She was stabbed in the heart," Melody said. Every time she closed her eyes, she could see that poor woman's body laying behind the dumpster. "Someone stabbed her just once, so they had to have known what they were doing. I'm betting that the person had some kind of training—medical or even military."

"That's why I'm your lead suspect," he said. "The stabbing through the heart signifies a murder of passion—even someone who was in love with her, and I have that military background you were talking about."

"Yes," she admitted. "That makes you my top suspect."

"Well, I hate to burst your bubble, Melody, but I was never in love with her. Hell, I tolerated being with Ginger, especially toward the end of our relationship. Honestly, I was stuck in a rut and didn't want to be alone, so I just rode out my time with her. Maybe that makes me an asshole, but I just couldn't bring myself to break up with her. I wanted to help fix her and I knew that pushing her out of my life wasn't the way to help her quit drinking. I just couldn't take anymore, so we broke up, and well, that was the day that she left me, taking everything from the year that we spent together—including the furniture."

"And you're telling me that didn't make you mad enough to kill her?" Melody asked. Sure, she was being a pushy bitch, but she had to know that she was truly barking up the wrong tree before she'd be willing to give up her quest.

"Has anyone ever taken something from you or wasted your time?" he asked.

"Um, sure," she said. "Why?"

"Did you murder them?" he asked.

"No," she breathed. "Point taken. The question remains if you didn't kill Ginger, who did?"

"I don't know, but that's what I was hoping you might want to help me figure out. Whether my new lawyer thinks that this is a problem or not, I want to help find her killer. I owe Ginger at least that much. Plus, it would be nice to officially clear my name, you know?" he asked.

"Are you asking me to work this case with you?" she asked. "My boss won't allow that."

"Well, we just won't tell Joel about us working together," he said.

"You know Joel?" she asked.

"Yeah—he and I used to be on the force together when we started years ago." Shit—that meant that he knew Joel when she was dating him. There was no way that she'd ever admit to Axel that she was fucking her boss back then. It wasn't any of his business.

"Right, well, Joel has a way of figuring things out that you're trying to keep a secret," she mumbled. At least, that was her experience with him. Every time she stepped a toe out of bounds, crossing the imaginary line between right and wrong, her boss found out and she was put on disciplinary probation.

"How about you handle your investigation and I handle my own?" he asked. Melody looked him over as if trying to decide if that was a good idea or not. If he was guilty, he could be playing her and if he was innocent, he could help her find the real murderer so that Ginger can rest in peace. She didn't know the woman, but she wanted that for her. From what she was finding out about Ginger, she hadn't always had an easy life, and that made Melody sad for her.

"Fine," she agreed. "We'll both work the case and see what we can come up with. But for the record, you're still at the top of my suspect list."

He chuckled, "Well, this is going to be fun," he said. "I'm guessing that our game of twenty questions is up?" he asked.

"Yep," she said. The waitress brought the breakfasts and she thanked her, handing the woman back her plate. "Can you wrap this up to go?" she said. "Sorry, but I've got to get to work." The woman didn't look very happy about Melody's change of plans but nodded and took back her plate.

As soon as the waitress disappeared, Axel leaned over the table and whispered, "She's totally going to spit in your food."

She giggled, "That's fine," she whispered back. "I'm taking it in as a peace offering to Joel. He loves breakfast." God, she shouldn't have said that last part. From Axel's expression, he was just as surprised that she said it too.

"How would you know that about your boss?" he asked.

"Long story," she breathed. He looked to be waiting her out and the waitress reappeared just in time with her to-go bag of food. She handed the woman some cash, thanked her, and stood.

"Another time," she said, shrugging down at Axel. "Enjoy your breakfast. I'll be in touch," she said. Melody didn't wait for him to respond, just turned to leave the little diner. She'd need to watch what she said to her number one suspect. The last thing she needed was for him to find out too much about her life. It needed to be the other way around and that's what Melody was headed downtown to figure out now. She needed to do some more research about Axel Lopez, but first, she was going to give Joel her peace offering to throw him off her trail. She didn't need her boss to know that she wasn't giving up researching Axel—or that they were possibly secretly working together to find Ginger's murderer. She just hoped like hell that the pancakes were good enough to do the trick, otherwise, she'd be looking for a new job, and that wouldn't help her latest victim to rest in peace.

AXEL

Axel headed into his office and found his partner, Hart sitting behind his desk. "Brought you back a little gift from Mexico," he said, holding up a bottle of tequila. "It even has the worm—you know, to test if you're a pussy or not." Axel took the bottle from his friend and thanked him.

"You guys didn't have to get me anything on your honeymoon," he said.

"Well, my new bride insisted," he said. "Besides, I had to let that woman out of bed once in a while," he teased. Axel rolled his eyes and sat down behind his desk.

"Glad you two had a good time," he said.

"Thanks," Hart said. "And thanks for holding down the fort around here while I was gone. Two weeks was a lot to ask you to take on. So, fill me in. I'm here to work my ass off to catch up." Their client cases had almost doubled in the last month and while Axel was happy that their name was getting out there, he was ready for a bit of a break.

"We have five cases going right now. Three more potential ones, if I can land them." He handed Hart the files and gave him a minute to look through them. They had an agreement that Hart would get first pick of cases and that was fine with him because Axel didn't give a fuck what cases he got. He just wanted to do his job and possibly help some people while getting paid.

"I'll take these three, lighten up your week a bit," he said.

"Thanks, man," Axel said, taking back the two files that were going to be his responsibility. "I could use a break." He knew that he was going to have to come clean with Hart about everything that was going on with Ginger, he just hated having to do it first thing after his partner got back.

"You all right?" Hart asked as if on cue.

"No," Axel admitted. "Ginger and I broke up last week," he said, easing into the truth.

"Well, I won't sit here and pretend to be sorry. I never really liked that woman. If you ask me, she needed to go to rehab to get some help. Tell me you dropped her ass off at rehab," Hart insisted. Maybe if he had, Ginger would still be alive, but at the time, the thought hadn't crossed his mind.

"No," Axel said. "I didn't drop her off at rehab, but you aren't wrong. She needed some help, and I was just too angry to help her find it. Maybe I could have even saved her life, if I just got over myself, man," he said.

"Wait—Ginger is dead?" Hart asked. "How? Was it the drinking?"

"Don't know. I'm guessing it was the stab wound to her heart that did it though," Axel joked.

"Fuck," Hart spat. "Tell me that you didn't fucking kill your ex, man."

"No," he breathed. "Why is everyone asking me that question?" he asked.

"Stabbing someone in the heart is a crime of passion, and well, you two were together," Hart explained.

"Right, but I wasn't in love with her," he said. "It's hard to love a drunk and well, Ginger showed her true colors early on. I just thought that I could fix her, you know—save her even. Instead, she's ended up dead and I'm the number one suspect in the case."

"What?" Hart spat. "You mean you've been called in for questioning?" he asked.

"Yep, last night, and I guess this morning, but that was an informal interview over breakfast," Axel said.

Hart groaned and dramatically threw his head back. "Tell me you didn't sleep with the cop who questioned you."

"Who says that she was even a she?" Axel asked.

"Was the cop a woman?" Hart asked.

"Yep," Axel admitted.

"Tell me you didn't fucking sleep with her, man," Hart repeated.

"I didn't," Axel said. "She steaked out my place all night and well, I called her on it. I've already been questioned and cleared last night. Savage had Razor meet me down at the station and I've got an alibi for the night of her murder. I was at Savage Hell that night and at least a dozen guys will testify that they saw me there."

"I fucking hate that guy," Hart admitted. "Razor is a prick."

"Yeah, but he's a good lawyer and prick or not, he got me out of the jam I was in," Axel said.

"Is it the truth—about you being at Savage Hell that night?" Hart asked. He was a part of Savage Hell, and he knew that their brothers would do just about anything to help another brother out.

"Yeah," Axel breathed. "It's the truth. That was the day that we broke up and the thought of going home to an empty apartment didn't sit right with me, so I decided to head into the bar and have a few beers to drown my sorrows."

"Well, thank God for that," Hart grumbled. "So, why was this sexy cop sitting in front of your place, if you were released?"

"Who said she was sexy?" Axel asked.

"Is she?" Hart questioned.

Axel sighed, "Yes," he admitted. "Try to focus, here, man," he insisted.

"Right," Hart mumbled. "So, why was she sitting out in front of your apartment?"

"Because she doesn't believe that I'm innocent. She said that I'm still at the top of her suspect list," Axel said.

"Shit," Hart growled. "What the hell are you going to do about that?" he asked.

"Well, I did the only thing I could think of—went out to breakfast with her." Hart looked Axel over as if he had lost his ever-loving mind, and maybe he had.

"You're one crazy fucker," Hart said. "You took a woman who believes that you're a cold-blooded killer out to breakfast?"

"Yep," he said. "I figured that I could answer her questions and maybe get her to believe that I didn't kill Ginger, because I plan on figuring out who did kill my ex."

"You didn't think to call Razor and ask him to be present for this questioning?" Hart asked. He had thought about it but decided against it. He needed Melody to believe him and showing up with his lawyer in tow would only have him looking guilty as hell in her eyes.

"No," Axel lied. "I didn't want to spook her. Besides, it was off the record questioning."

"You're not that stupid, man," Hart griped. "You know better."

"Yeah," he said. "I do, and that's why I didn't say anything that can get me into trouble."

"Does the sexy woman cop believe your innocence now?" Hart asked.

"No," Axel admitted, listening to a string of curses come from his best friend. "But she's agreed to share information with me, in exchange for anything that I might find out about the case."

"I'm sure she'll do just that," Hart said. "I mean, why wouldn't she share information with the man who she believes is the number one suspect in her murder case. That makes complete sense."

"Your sarcasm isn't necessary," Axel mumbled.

"I'm not sure that you're thinking correctly, man. Maybe you should stop thinking with your dick for long enough to figure out that she's playing you," Hart said.

"Melody wouldn't do that," Axel said. "She seems to play by the rules."

"What's her name?" Hart asked. He pulled his laptop open and started typing and Axel groaned.

"You're going to do some research, aren't you?" Axel asked.

"Yep." Hart was damn good at researching people. If someone was hiding something, his partner could weed it out in no time. "Her name," Hart growled.

"Melody Valentine," Axel reluctantly admitted. If he didn't tell Hart her name, he'd just use other means to find it out. Hell, he wouldn't put it past his partner to just walk into the precinct and demand to know where some chick named Melody was. That was the last thing that Axel needed.

"Fuck—even her name sounds like sex on a stick. You weren't getting any red flags to steer clear of this woman, man?" Hart asked.

"Shut the fuck up and just research her," Axel griped. "I've got to head out to talk with one of our new potential clients about their home security system. It's part of a test I think that they are doing to make sure that we're on the up and up and as good as I've promised them that we are. Let me know what you find out about Melody."

"Will do," Hart barked. "But for the time being, promise me that you'll steer clear of her. If she calls, don't even answer her fucking calls."

"Sure," Axel lied. There was no way that he'd avoid Melody's calls because she could have some news about Ginger's true murderer, and there wasn't anything that he wouldn't do to clear his name.

It had been a long fucking day and all Axel wanted to do was down a few beers and call it a night. He had managed to take a few minutes out of his schedule to run to the local furniture store and purchase a new bed and even a sofa and kitchen table and chairs. It was the first time that he had ever purchased furniture brand new and damn if that didn't make him feel like a responsible adult.

After his parents' deaths, he and his brother could barely make ends meet. His little brother was in school, and that was where he planned on keeping him. Axel worked two jobs and wasn't around a whole lot, but he managed to put food on the table and clothes on his brother's back as he grew. But nothing was ever new. Everything that they owned came second hand, and he never really cared about any of that. But now, he wanted a fresh start and with his and Hart's business taking off and doing well, he could finally have it.

He walked into Savage Hell and found his partner sitting at the bar with his new wife, Shannon. "Just the man I need to see," Hart said.

"Oh?" Axel asked. "I take it you have some news for me then?"

"Yep," Hart said.

"Well, let me at least hug my favorite woman before you get started," Axel insisted, pulling Shannon up from her barstool and into his arms. "How was the honeymoon?" he asked.

Shannon looked back at her husband and sighed. "Wonderful," she gushed. Axel released her and she went right back to Hart's side.

"We got a babysitter for the night and decided to come to the bar for a little alone time," Hart said.

Axel looked his friend over. "You and I have very different opinions about what alone time is, man," he teased, causing Shannon to giggle.

"I've been promised that we will only be here for an hour—just long enough for Jackson to tell you about this sexy policewoman he keeps mentioning." She shot her husband a look and now it was Axel's turn to laugh.

"What?" Hart growled. "What the hell did I do now?"

"I'm sure that he'll figure out how he's already fucked up," Axel promised. "You've only been home for a day, man," he chided. "So, what have you dug up on her?" Axel asked.

"She's a troublemaker. Melody Valentine has been on disciplinary probation a handful of times. She doesn't like to follow the rules and her boss doesn't seem to have the balls to fire her," Hart said.

"He's got the balls," Axel said. "I know her boss personally. We came up through the department together. He's tough as nails, so there has to be another reason why he won't fire her for going against the grain that way."

"He's sleeping with her," Shannon offered.

"He's a captain now and Joel was a stickler for rules. He'd never sleep with his underling," Axel insisted.

"It would explain why he never cut her loose," Hart said, agreeing with his new wife. "Good job, honey, I think you figured out our mystery. Melody is sleeping with her boss. Now, all we have to do is get her fired and she won't be on this case anymore. You won't have to watch your back." Hart's smile faded when he looked back at Axel to find him shaking his head at him.

"No," Axel said. "I won't get her fired. That will just make me look like I'm guilty as hell. You keep the information that you found to yourself. If I need it, I'll come to you, but I want this investigation run on the up and up because when they find Ginger's killer, I don't want anything to keep the cops from throwing him or her into prison."

"I think it's a man," Shannon offered. "Whoever did it would have to be strong enough to get the knife through bone and into her heart."

"Plus, unless Ginger was into women, I'd agree that it had

to be a guy. I said it earlier, and I'll say it again. It was a crime of passion and whoever did it loved her or believed that he was in love with her. Was your woman a lesbian and you never told us?" Hart asked.

"No," Axel said.

"Could she have been sleeping around on you?" Shannon asked. He shot Hart a look and nodded.

"Yeah," Axel admitted. "She liked to drink too much and then hit on the guys in the club. The only reason they didn't take her up on her offers was that they're my brothers. No one would touch my Ol'lady. But that doesn't mean that she didn't ask around at other bars and that some guy wouldn't give a fuck if she was with me or not."

"Shit," Hart said. "I think that killer might have been fucking your girl on the side, man." Axel didn't want to admit it, but he was starting to believe the same thing. The question was—who?

The bar grew quiet as all the bikers turned to look over the woman who had just walked into their club. She must have been new because most of the guys were staring with their mouths open as if they wanted a taste of her.

"Fuck," Hart breathed. "It's her. I recognize her from her picture."

"God damnit," Axel growled, turning to watch Melody look around the bar. She was trying to find him; he could tell the moment she spotted him. The detective was in full-on work mode right now and he was wondering what fresh hell she was about to deliver.

Melody crossed the bar, all eyes still on her, and nodded to him. "Axel," she said.

"What the fuck are you doing at my club, Detective?" he asked.

"I told you to call me Melody," she corrected.

"Right, but I have a feeling that you're here on business, and I'd like to skip right to the formalities," Axel insisted.

"Sure," she said. "Ah—Mr. Razor," Melody said as the big biker pushed his way into their tiny corner of the room. "I'm assuming that you're here to protect your client, but good news—there is no need. Mr. Lopez has been completely cleared as a suspect on our case."

"How?" Axel asked. "You told me this morning that I was still at the top of your suspect list."

Razor's growl filled the bar. "You met with her behind my back?" he asked. "I told you to steer clear of the detective and this case."

"I'm afraid that his going against your trusted council is my fault," Melody covered. "You see, I showed up at Axel's place this morning and well, I asked him to have breakfast with me. We talked, off record, and that actually helped me to clear his name."

"How so?" Axel asked.

"Well, remember when you said that I never told you about how Ginger died?" she said.

"Yes," Axel breathed.

"I never told you where she died either. Her body was found behind a dumpster, and I decided to go have another look at the crime scene. That's when I realized that the bar on the corner of the alley had cameras that actually had eyes on the dumpster. I realized that I could subpoena the camera's footage if they refused to give it to me, but that wasn't necessary. The owner fully cooperated and well, I found what I was looking for."

"You know who the killer is?" Razor asked.

"No," she said. "The footage was blurry. Forensics is trying to clean it up, but it's a long, tedious process. What I do know is that she wasn't killed in that alley. Someone dragged her dead body to where we found it and left it behind the dumpster."

"I don't understand how that clears my name," Axel said.

"You don't fit the guy's build. You're a lot bigger than he is and well, his hair was longer. Have you had a haircut in the past week?" she asked.

"No," Axel said. "Being in the military, I never have had long hair. I keep it short and tight, just like the old days."

"He's not lying," Hart said. "I can vouch that he's always had that same pussy haircut," he teased, causing her to laugh. Yeah, the last thing Axel needed was his best friend making fun of him, but he'd let that one slide.

"This is Hart and his new wife, Shannon. Hart and I are business partners and he's also an ex-cop," Axel explained.

"You did look familiar," Melody said. "Have we met before?"

"No," Hart said. "I'm pretty sure that I would have

remembered." Shannon poked her husband in the ribs and now it was Axel's turn to laugh.

"Good to meet you, Melody," Shannon said. "But I think that it's time to get my husband home so that we can have our first married fight."

Hart bobbed his eyebrows at his new wife. "I hear that married make-up sex is quite the rage," he teased. Shannon slapped at his arm as if protesting the idea, but everyone could see the blush that tinted her cheeks at her husband's outrageous suggestion. Shannon grabbed her husband's hand and started dragging him out of the bar.

"See you in the morning," Hart said, on his way past Axel. "Good to meet you," he breathed as they passed Melody. She nodded and took the stool that Hart had just vacated.

"Sure, make yourself at home," he offered.

"I just brought you really good news, Axel. The least you can do is buy me a beer," she said.

"I'd be happy to, but I had you pegged as a wine drinker," he teased.

"Well, I do love my red wine," she admitted. "But I'm a beer drinker to my core. I've been drinking beer with my dad since before it was legal for me to do so."

"Wow, Detective," Axel feigned shock. "You mean to say that you broke the law? I'm betting that you've been breaking rules for some time now. Would I be correct?" he asked. He knew from Hart's research that he had done on her that she was a rule breaker.

"I'm assuming you did some research on me too," she said, not really seeming angry.

"Why do you sound fine with that?" he asked.

"Because I spent the morning after I left the diner researching you. You're quite a rule breaker yourself," she said.

"I plead the fifth," he teased, causing her to laugh. Bowie brought the two of them each a beer and smiled and nodded at her when she thanked him.

"Wow," she breathed, taking a big sip of her beer. "Do all of the guys look like you in here?"

"Look like me?" he asked. "What does that mean?"

"Well, you all got the big, sexy, biker look down—except for Razor. He's just a hulk. Do they put something in the beer?"

He chuckled, "So, you think I'm sexy?" he asked, scooting a little closer to her.

"What?" she asked. He could tell that she was rethinking everything that she had just said to him. "When did I say that?"

"When you asked if all the guys look like me," he reminded. "You said that I'm a big, sexy biker if I remember correctly." He smugly sipped his beer, waiting for her to refute him.

"Fine," she spat. "I think you're sexy, but that doesn't matter because you're involved in the case that I'm investigating, and I won't fuck things up. I'm sure that you found how many times I've been on disciplinary probation in the past two years. I won't go through that again because sooner or later, my boss is going to lose it and let me go."

"First, I thought that I wasn't involved in the case any longer. You said I wasn't a suspect," he said.

"Right, but you're still involved. You're the murdered woman's ex-boyfriend. That fact won't change," she said. "What was the second part of your question?" she asked.

"Second part?" he asked.

"Yeah, you said, 'First' before you asked me your question. That usually implies that you have a second question."

"Oh," he said. She was right, he was going to ask her a second question, but now that he had thought it over, he was regretting using the word, "First" at all. It was best to just ask her and get it over with. "Are you sleeping with Joel?" he asked, just ripping off the band-aid.

Melody choked on the swallow of beer that she had just taken. "What?" she asked. "You think I'm sleeping with my boss?"

"No," he said. "Actually, my partner did the research on you this morning. I wasn't looking for information, but he wanted to know what we were up against. That's just his way. When he mentioned all of the times that you were on probation at work, we wondered why you weren't just fired. That's when his new wife said that you were probably sleeping with your boss."

"Shit," she said, wiping the beer from her chin. "Leave it to another woman to figure that kind of shit out."

"So, it's true?" he asked. He wasn't sure how he felt about her admission. Hadn't she just called him sexy?

"No," she breathed. "I had a relationship with Joel, that part is true. And maybe that's why Joel hasn't fired my ass yet. But we haven't been together in years since he became my boss actually. When I started as a young cop, I met Joel. He worked at another precinct, and we hit it off while we were working a case together. He wasn't my boss then. Hell, he wasn't even my superior. We spent four months together and we were practically living with each other, but then, he found out that he was going to be my boss. He told me that he wasn't going to take the promotion, and I couldn't let him do that. He had to take it because I knew that he was going to be an awesome captain and I couldn't let our relationship hold him back. I also wouldn't give up the chance to make detective, and in order to be promoted, I had to accept the job working under Joel. So, I did the only thing that I could think to do—broke things off with him."

"Wow," Axel breathed. "Just like that? You kicked him to the curb after four months together?"

"Yep," she admitted. "I know that makes me sound like a cold-hearted bitch, but I did it for him. He wanted things that I didn't—marriage, kids, the house with the white picket fence. I wasn't ready for any of that, so I honestly did him a favor."

"Did you love him?" Axel asked.

She took another sip of her beer and shook her head. "I thought that I did, but after we broke up, I realized that I didn't. I got over him quickly and if I was in love with him, would I have been able to do that?"

"But he still loves you, doesn't he?" Axel said, taking a guess. "That's why he doesn't fire you and puts up with you breaking the rules."

"Yes," she whispered. "And I'm a complete asshole for putting him in the positions that I do. I know that he still has feelings for me and well, I use them to push the envelope with him. Does that make me a bitch?" she asked.

"Yes," he admitted.

She laughed, "I agree with you, actually. That's why I needed to sneak around when watching you. He told me to drop my pursuit of you in this case, but I just couldn't. I needed to know for sure."

"And now, you're sure?" he asked.

"I think so," Melody agreed. "I'm sure for now if that helps." It didn't, but he'd worry about all of that later.

"Hey, Axel," Spider said, joining them at the bar. "Who's your new friend?" he asked. Spider was one of the new guys patched in at Savage Hell and he seemed like a decent guy.

"Name's Melody," the detective said. "You are?"

"Spider," he said, holding out his hand to her.

"Do any of you guys have normal names?" she mumbled under her breath.

"Biker names are real names," Axel insisted.

"I haven't seen Ginger around," Spider said. "You two still together?"

"Ginger's dead," Melody said. She turned to face Spider

and Axel wondered why she'd just blurt out the bad news as she had. "You didn't hear?"

"Um, no," Spider said. "That's awful. I'm sorry, man," he said, looking around Melody to where Axel sat.

"Thanks," Axel breathed.

"How'd it happen?" Spider asked.

"She was murdered," Melody answered for him. "I'm surprised you didn't hear about it around here. I mean, I'm betting that the guys have been talking about it since my officers were here questioning everyone. Ginger was a regular here, right?" she asked Axel.

"Yes," he said. "When I was here, she was with me, usually."

"So, you could even say that she was one of your own, right?" she asked.

"Yes," Axel said again. "She was one of us."

"Then, why wouldn't Spider here know about Ginger being murdered?" she asked.

"I haven't been in for a bit," Spider said as in defense. "You're a cop?" he asked.

"I'm the detective handling the case," Melody said. "Have you been out of town, Spider?" she asked. Why was she asking Spider so many questions? It was almost as though she believed he was a suspect, but Axel knew that they were all suspects since they all knew Ginger. She was playing things just the way that he would have.

"Out of town," he repeated. "Um, no. I've just been busy, is all." Melody shot Axel a look and he could tell that she didn't believe a word that he was saying. Axel wasn't sure that he believed Spider either. The guy seemed too nervous, especially since finding out that she was a police detective. He even seemed a bit jumpy—like he couldn't wait to get out of there.

"I'm really sorry to hear about Ginger, man," Spider said to Axel. "I'm going to head out. You two have a good night." He nodded at Melody and started for the door to leave.

"I don't trust that one," Melody breathed.

"Spider seems pretty harmless," Axel defended.

"It's the shy, quiet, harmless ones you have to watch, Axel. You should know that better than anyone," she said.

"Right, but Spider really didn't even know Ginger," Axel insisted. "Why would he want to stab her in the heart?"

She shot him a look and rolled her eyes. "Are you sure that Ginger and Spider didn't know each other? I mean, you said yourself that she liked to get drunk and hit on guys at the bar."

"Sure, but nothing ever came of it. The guys wouldn't do that," he assured.

"How long has Spider been a part of the club?" she asked.

"He's a new patch in," Axel said. "About a year, I'm guessing."

"So, you really don't know him that well," Melody said.

"No," Axel said. "I don't know Spider that well. But I can say that I never saw him and Ginger hanging out together. She never mentioned him, or anything like that, if it helps."

She shrugged and took another drink of her beer. "I just

like being thorough, Axel. If you didn't kill Ginger, who did?" she asked.

"No clue," he said. "But I'd still like to help you figure it out—in a non-official capacity. I'm going to use my resources at my agency to dig around, and if I find anything, I'll be in touch."

"You're still willing to help out even though you are no longer a suspect?" she asked.

"Of course," he agreed. "I was with Ginger for a year and even though I wasn't in love with her, I still cared about her. I'd like to help."

"All right, but this is completely off the record. If Joel finds out that I've let a civilian in on this case, he'll have my badge." Axel smirked over at her, and she giggled. They both knew that Joel wouldn't fire her—especially if he was still in love with her as she suspected.

"How about I meet you back here tomorrow night for an update? Joel will never suspect that I'm coming in here to meet you," she offered.

"Sounds good," Axel said. "I'll be here—same spot and all." Melody finished her beer and got up to leave. He almost wanted to ask her to stay, but that would be a fucking awful mistake. She wasn't the type of woman he usually asked to come home with him, and for some reason, that made him want to shake things up a bit.

MELODY

Joel was waiting for her in her little cubby once she got into the office the next morning. "Hey boss," she said, pasting on her best smile. Melody could almost feel his bad mood and that had her worried. It wasn't like Joel to be in a shitty mood usually—unless she did something to piss him off.

"What's up?" she asked.

"How about you tell me?" he insisted. Red flags were going up all around her. This was usually the part where she spilled her guts, telling Joel everything, and giving him more information than he originally had. She wasn't going to fall for his tricks again this time and tell him that she was secretly planning on working with Axel Lopez and his detective agency to solve Ginger's case.

"Not sure what you're talking about," she said.

He sunk into her chair, looking up at her as if trying to wait her out. "I thought we agreed that Axel Lopez wasn't a suspect anymore when he and his lawyer left here two days ago."

"Right," she said. "His lawyer said that he had an alibi and you believed him. But I never agreed that Lopez wasn't a suspect anymore."

"So, you did your own research on him?" Joel asked.

"Yes, I did. That's how I found the actual footage of a man dragging Ginger's body into that alley and putting it behind the dumpster. And it's also how I know that Lopez isn't a suspect anymore."

"How so?" Joel asked.

"Take a look at the surveillance footage and you'll be able to see for yourself," she said. Melody pulled up the video on her phone and handed it to Joel. He watched the video twice and then handed it back to her.

"Not the right build," he said. "Lopez is a lot bigger than that guy. We suspected that she wasn't killed in that spot. So, the killer murdered her someplace else and then dragged her body to the alley. That fits with what forensics found."

"I know," Melody said. "Now, all we have to do is get them to clean up that picture, and we'll have our guy."

"Have you already assigned them that task or do I need to jump on that?" Joel asked.

"Already done, boss," she said.

"I really wish you'd stop calling me that, Melody," he said.

"But you're my boss and calling you that reminds me of that fact," she said.

"Right," he said, standing. "Well, I'll expect to be kept in the loop from now on. You tell Lopez that he's officially cleared?"

"Yes," she said. As the lead detective on the case, that would fall under her jurisdiction. "I found him last night and told him on my way home from work."

Joel looked her over as though he wanted to say something and then nodded. "Good work, Melody," he breathed.

"Thanks, boss," she said. Joel huffed out his breath and walked out of her tiny cubical. All in all, that went pretty well, but she still worried that he'd find out that she was working with Axel to figure out who the shadowy figure was in the video. Her only hope was that they'd find the killer before Joel found out that she had basically employed a civilian to help her solve her case.

Melody parked in the back of the lot at Savage Hell, not wanting to draw too much attention to herself. She knew that she already stood out as the only car in the lot. Most of the vehicles there were bikes and even a few pick-up trucks, but no sedans. She stuck out like a sore thumb, and there wasn't a thing she could do about it.

She walked into the bar and looked around for any sign of Axel, finding him playing darts with Razor in the other guy who said he was his business partner. She thought his name was Hart, but she could be wrong. Axel spotted her and waved her back. She weaved her way through the mass of bikers in the bar and finally got back to Axel and his friends.

"Hey," he said, looking her over. "You look different tonight." She nodded, not about to admit that she had run by her place to change out of her work clothes and into her tightest jeans and t-shirt she could find. She paired the outfit with some black leather boots and was pretty happy with herself. She looked the part and loved the feeling of going undercover again. Melody used to take any undercover case that she could get her hands on, but lately, they were few and far between. Most of the undercover cases were given out to the men since that was what was needed. She missed the good old days of getting dressed up and playing a part. This little undercover operation that she and Axel had going on was just what she needed. It gave her an excuse to pull her old stuff from the closet and play dress up. She even did her make-up and gave herself some big hair, just like the old days. Yeah—she was really getting into the part.

"I thought that I'd have a little bit of fun," she admitted. "Besides, I'm pretty sure that my work clothes scream, 'She's a cop,' and that's the last thing I need in here. I'm betting that most of your guys would avoid me if they thought that I was a police detective."

"Oh, I don't know," Razor said, looking her over, giving her the same attention that Axel just had. The only difference was when Axel looked at her the way that he was, it made her hot. When Razor did, she wanted to punch him in the nut sac. "I think that you look hot. I'd ask you out."

"Are you asking me out?" she asked.

"Sure—want to go out with me, detective?" he asked. He was too smug for her. Hell, she knew a lot of men like Razor. Most of them were on the force and she usually did her best to steer clear of them. It was for the best.

"No," she breathed. "You aren't my type, Razor," she said.

"Ouch," Razor said, holding his heart, feigning hurt. "That hurt."

"You'll have to excuse him," Hart said. "Razor doesn't get turned down very often. It's nice to see you knock him down a few pegs."

"She did not knock me down a few pegs," Razor insisted. "I'm just surprised is all."

"Why does my turning you down surprise you?" she asked.

"Because you are just my type, so I thought you'd feel the same way about me. I guess I had you pegged all wrong. You do like men, right?"

"Why, because I turned you down so I must be a lesbian?" she asked. "Really, Razor? You're an ass and I won't even answer your question." Melody turned to Axel and smiled. "Want to buy me a beer?" she asked.

"Love to," Axel agreed. "Mind if Hart joins us? We have some information you might want to hear." Melody nodded and followed the two of them over to the bar. She was hoping that they'd have a lead because she had come up with nothing after a full day of digging.

The bartender got them set up at the end of the bar, where things were a little quieter and a bit more private. "You have news?" she asked.

"Yes," Axel said. "We did a bit of digging and talked to one of Ginger's friends. She was living with Ginger before I met her, and she moved into my place. Ginger moved in quickly and didn't leave things on good terms with her old roommate, so I never met her before today."

"Did she know that Ginger had been murdered?" Melody asked. She was a bit hurt that they hadn't called her to go talk to the former roommate with them, but why would they? She didn't make any promises to work together on this case, and they didn't make her any promises either.

"No," Hart said. "She was pretty upset, too."

"She did give us some information that might be helpful," Axel said. "See, I wore my cut, and she recognized the Royal Bastard patch on my back."

"Now you've lost me," she said. "First, what's a cut?"

"It's our leathers. Some of us wear a vest, some wear jackets," Hart explained. "It was cold enough today that Axel wore his jacket, and the back has this patch," Hart said, turning around to give her a look at the Royal Bastards patch that took up the entire back of it.

"I see," she said. "I thought that your club was called Savage Hell, like the bar," she said.

"We are," Axel said. "Savage hell is the name of our little

Axel's Grind

chapter here in Huntsville, but we're part of the Royal Bastards."

"Got it," she said, although, she still felt a bit mixed up. She never had any idea that biker clubs were so complicated. "So, getting back to this former roommate, what does it matter that she recognized your patch?"

"She recognized the patch because Ginger was dating a guy who wore a jacket like mine, just before she moved into my place," Axel said.

"You didn't know that Ginger was dating someone before you?" Melody asked.

"No," he said. "And I certainly didn't know that she was seeing someone from my club," Axel grumbled.

"And you think that the guy she was seeing, from your club, might be our murderer?" Melody asked. It was a long shot, but honestly, that was more than she had to go on.

"Possibly," Hart said.

"Well, did she give you a description of the guy? Would she be willing to come down here to see if she could point him out?" Melody asked.

"We didn't ask. She kicked us out as soon as we told her that Ginger was dead. She said that she needed to be alone, and well, we knew our time was up," Hart said. "We didn't need her calling the police if we refused to leave, so we took off," Axel said.

"Good thinking," she said. "I think I'll go by her place in the morning and ask her how she feels about coming down here to take a look at your guys. If she can point out Ginger's old flame, we might be able to get some answers."

"Thanks," Axel said. "I don't think that us showing up at her place again will do any good. I have a feeling that she'll just tell us to leave."

"Any clue as to who this guy might be?" she asked.

"No," Axel said. "No clue. For all we know, he might not still be here. Sometimes guys move on and join another Royal Bastards in another city."

"Can Savage get us a list of everyone who's been patched in or left in the last eighteen months?" Hart asked.

Axel shrugged, "Most likely, but I'll ask him."

"Good, that will give us a starting point," Melody said. "Now, if you boys will excuse me, I need to head home. I have a hot bath and bed calling my name. It's been a damn long day."

"I'll walk you out," Axel offered. "You shouldn't head out by yourself—this is a biker bar, after all," he teased.

"Right," she said. "I hear that they're pretty seedy places and that the bikers can get a bit rough."

"Whoever told you that isn't wrong," Hart joked. "Good seeing you again, Melody. We'll be in touch in the morning once we can get the list from Savage."

"I appreciate that," Melody said. "Good to see you too, Hart."

She followed Axel out of the bar and breathed in the cool air once they got outside. "Oh, that's so much better," she said. "It was pretty stuffy in there," she said.

"Yeah, it's usually like that," Axel said. "It's worse in the summer."

"I guess I'm glad that it's winter then," she said. "And I never thought that I'd ever say that."

He chuckled. "Where did you park?" he asked

"Back of the lot, in the corner," she said. "I didn't want to stand out with my sedan parked in a sea of bikes."

"Yeah, we don't get many sedans back here," he agreed. He walked her back to her car, and she turned to thank him, noting the way his smile fell. "You can't leave," he said.

"Why not?" she asked. "Are you okay?"

"I am, but your tires aren't," he said. "Someone has slashed your tires." Axel rounded her car and shook his head at the flat tires.

"Who would do that?" she asked.

"Don't know, but I'm guessing you didn't hide away well enough back here. It's either someone trying to send you a message or a random act done by some asshole."

"Who would want to send me a message?" she asked.

He looked over the top of the car at her. "Someone who doesn't want you solving the case. Hell, if Ginger's old roommate is correct, and she was dating a guy from Savage Hell, he might be in the bar right now. What if he's sending you the message?"

"I'm going to have to call this in," she said.

"And alert your boss to the fact that you were here meeting with Hart and me about the case?" Axel asked.

"I won't tell him that part. I'll simply tell Joel that I was here having a little fun—blowing off steam" she defended.

"And your boss will believe that you blow off steam and hang out at biker bars?" Axel asked. Melody felt a bit defeated. She wasn't sure what to do.

"What the hell am I supposed to do?" she whispered.

"Leave your car here and I'll have it towed into a friend's shop and he'll replace the tires," he offered. He knew that Cillian would take care of Melody, no questions asked.

"Will you run me home?" she asked.

"You think it's safe for you to go home alone?" Axel asked.

"Why wouldn't it be?" Melody questioned.

"If this was done on purpose, whoever is coming for you might be stalking your place already. It might not be safe for you to stay alone," he insisted.

"I'm a cop," she mumbled. "I think that I can handle a tire slasher."

"It always starts with tire slashing and goes south from there." Axel grabbed her hand into his own. "Let me stay with you," he offered. "I can sleep on the couch. Two cops are better than one, right?" He wasn't wrong. Two cops under one roof would make better odds if someone came snooping around her place. Melody looked back at her car and shook her head.

"Fine," she agreed. "You can stay with me, but in the morning, I'm coming back here and talking to Savage. He has security cameras, I've seen them. I'll need to see if he has any that might have caught who did this to my car tires."

"I'll come back here with you in the morning, take care of your car, and talk to Savage about members," Axel offered.

"All right," she said. "Please tell me that one of those pick-up trucks is yours," she said.

"You're not into bikes?" he asked.

"I am, just not when it's this cold," she said.

"Well, lucky for you, I'm that pick-up over there in the front of the side entrance." He nodded to where his truck sat, and she let out her breath.

"Good," she said. "Thanks." She followed him over to his truck and all she could do was think about the fact that he was going to be sleeping over at her place tonight. She almost wanted to laugh at the irony of it all. Just last night, she thought that he was a murderer, and now, she was going to allow him to sleep on her sofa.

AXEL

Axel texted Hart as soon as he got to Melody's place, letting him know what was going on. Hart assured him that he'd secure her car and let Savage know what happened. Now, all he had to do was get through a night on Melody's couch, and not wake up with a raging boner the next morning. He had a feeling that an erection wasn't something he should bring to the breakfast table.

"You really think that whoever slashed my tires is involved in Ginger's murder?" she asked. He had no clue, but he didn't feel like taking any chances.

"I don't know," he admitted. "I just find it strange that we're getting closer to the truth, asking questions, and this happened."

"I feel the same way," she admitted. "Maybe it's not a coincidence, but I feel foolish having you sleep on my sofa. I can just lock myself in, and I have a gun," she said, nodding to her gun she had sat on the kitchen counter. "I think I can handle myself."

"I never said that you couldn't handle yourself, Melody," he said. "But maybe someone else watching your back might help you rest easier."

"I'm worried that we're doing the wrong thing by not calling this in," she said. "I feel like I'm lying to my boss, and I try to be as honest as possible with Joel."

"While I'm sure you feel guilty about not calling in your slashed tires, it's for the best. We don't know who we can and can't trust. Just let me take care of this, and then, we can figure out how to tell Joel that we're working together," Axel offered.

"Okay," she said. "I'm going to have a bath and head to bed. I have a spare room, so you don't really have to sleep on the sofa."

"Really?" he asked, sounding almost too excited about the fact that he wouldn't have to wake up with his back aching from her sofa.

"Yep," she said. "It's down the hall from mine, so if something happens, you'll be right there for me to protect," she teased.

"You're sure that you don't mind?" he asked. "I don't mind sleeping on the sofa," he lied.

She giggled, "You know, I'm finding it hard to believe you when you make that face every time you say it. My sofa isn't the most comfortable place to sleep. Besides, it's silly for you not to use my spare bed. Come on," she ordered. He followed her to her spare room and turned on the light.

"This will work," he said as she looked back over her shoulder to him. "Thanks. I have a bag in the trunk. I'll just grab it and will probably hit the sheets myself."

"You keep a to-go bag in your trunk?" she asked.

"Yeah," he said. "I know that sounds a bit strange, but it comes in handy when I get stuck on a stakeout."

"No, not strange at all," she said. "I get it. I do the same thing. If you need anything else, please let me know. The guest bathroom is right across the hallway and my room is two doors down. Feel free to help yourself to anything in the kitchen if you're hungry. Although, I'm not sure what you will find in the fridge."

"Thanks, Melody," he said. "I appreciate it." He watched as she disappeared down the hallway to her room and shut the door. Axel pulled his cell phone out of his pocket and quickly called Hart, wanting to fill him in on what happened.

Heart picked up after the first ring. "Tell me that she has some idea who slashed her tires," he demanded. This was why he was planning on waiting until morning to call Hart, but he knew that his friend would want to be filled in and that his earlier text wasn't going to be good enough.

"No clue," Axel said. "We didn't want to take any chances that it's not connected to the case, so I'm staying with her tonight."

"What?" Hart barked into the other end of the call. "Tell me that you're not going to fuck her, Axel. That would be a colossally bad idea since she's working the case, that until recently, you were the main suspect for."

"No, I'm sleeping in her guest room. It's just until we can figure out what's going on and who slashed her tires," Axel said. He was just going to conveniently leave out the part about finding her to be sexy as hell or that he'd already fantasized about her offering to share her bed with him. Hart didn't need to know that bit of information.

"You're telling me that you don't think that she's hot?" Hart asked.

"What—no, I don't think that she's hot," Axel growled. He heard her gasp before turning around to find Melody standing in the doorway of the spare room. "Shit got to go, man," Axel mumbled, ending the call.

"Listen," he said, crossing the room to stand in front of her.

She held up her hands, pressing them against his chest as he crowded her space. "No need to explain," she said. "I'm fine with the fact that you don't find me hot. In fact, it's for the best because we're working on the case together and everything."

"Melody," he whispered. Axel looked down at where her hands were still on his chest. "I didn't mean what I told Hart. He's being an ass and prying into my personal life. My finding you hot has nothing to do with him, so I told him what I had to in order to get him off my ass. I'm sorry that it upset you."

"You didn't upset me," she lied. "Wait—you find me hot?" she asked.

"I do," he admitted. "I mean, look at you," he said, looking her up and down. She was his walking wet dream, but he wasn't about to admit that to her. Not when they were both standing so close, and her hands were still on his pecks.

"Oh," she breathed. Melody suddenly realized that her hands were still on his body and quickly removed them. "I see."

"Melody," he said, reaching for her. She took a step back from him and pulled her robe tighter around her body.

"I just wanted to make sure that you had everything that you needed for the night," she said. Axel knew that there was going to be no talking about everything right now, and maybe that was for the best. They were both exhausted and maybe a good night's sleep might help them both think more clearly.

"I'm good," he said. "Thank you, Melody." She nodded and turned to go back down the hall to her bedroom. He waited until he heard her door shut before he flopped down onto the bed. It was going to be a damn long night, but some shut eye was just what he needed.

Axel's Grind

Axel woke up to the sound of glass breaking. He sat up and took just a second to figure out where the hell he was. "Hey," Melody whispered. "You awake?" she asked.

"I am," he breathed. "Is that you making all that noise?"

"No," she said. "I think that someone is in my house."

"You have your gun?" she asked.

"Yeah," he whispered. "You think we should call this in? You know, get the cops involved," he asked.

"I am the cops," she whisper shouted. "Now get up and watch my six while I find out who the fuck is in my house." He grabbed his pants and she looked back at him and sighed. "We don't have time for that. Just grab your gun."

He did as she ordered and followed her down the hall to the stairs. "Be careful," he whispered. He stayed close behind her as she made her way to the kitchen. He felt the cold air coming through the back door before he spotted the broken glass. From the look of it, there wasn't enough space for a person to squeeze through.

"I don't think anyone is in your house," he said. He turned on the light and found the back door busted, glass laying on the kitchen floor, and a brick laying in the middle of the mess.

"What's that paper on top of the brick?" she asked.

"I think that someone's left you a note," he said.

She grabbed a pair of sneakers that she kept by the back door, and carefully waded through the glass to pull the paper from the rubbish. "Here," she said. "I can't read it."

He took the note from her and opened it. "It says, 'You're going to die next, bitch,'" he read.

"Oh God," she breathed. "Why would someone do this?"

"Well, it's pretty clear," Axel said. "Someone is coming for you, just like they did Ginger."

"You think it's all linked?" she asked.

"I do," he said. "And I think that you need to call this in now, honey. This is the second thing to happen in the past few hours. Whoever is coming for you is doing so at warp speed. It's time to tell Joel."

"All right," she said. "You're right. I'm now involved in this case more than I should be." She put the note on the kitchen counter and grabbed her cell phone. "I'll call him now. Would you mind grabbing the broom from the pantry over there?"

"Sure," he agreed. He grabbed the broom and started sweeping up the glass as he listened in to her conversation with her boss. He didn't seem very happy about the situation, judging from the amount of yelling coming from the other end of the call.

Melody ended the call and tossed her cell phone onto the kitchen counter. "Shit," she grumbled. "That was a fucking awful idea. He's on his way here now with to uniforms. The last thing I need is for my boss to find me here with you, Axel." He understood that him being there with her might give her boss the wrong idea, but it still hurt to hear Melody say it.

"I'm not that bad, am I?" he teased.

"You aren't bad at all, Axel," she insisted, looking him over. "He'll just think that we're together."

"And you don't want him to think that because of the case or because you're ashamed to be seen with me?" he asked. Sure, he was trying to get some answers as to where he stood with her. He had admitted that she was hot, but she treated him like he had the plague most of the time that they were even in the same room.

"No," she said. "I'm not ashamed to be seen with you, Axel." Melody took the dustpan full of glass from him and dumped it into the kitchen garbage can. "This will have to go out so that no one cuts themselves." She was avoiding him, and he hated feeling as though he had been dismissed.

"Leave it," he growled as she started to pull the bag from the can. "Look at me, Melody," he ordered. She sighed and dropped the bag, turning to face him.

"Can't we do this later?" she asked. "You know, when you're not standing in my kitchen in your boxers and my boss isn't on his way over here?" Axel looked down his body and back up at her, giving her his best smile.

"My boxers are distracting you?" he asked.

"Yes," she hissed. "You're practically naked in my kitchen and that's distracting as hell." Hearing her admit that she was knocked a little off kilter seeing him in his boxers, actually gave him some sick, smug satisfaction.

"How about if I did this," he said, pulling her up against his body. "Is this distracting?"

"Yeah," she breathed, seeming to lose a bit of her fight.

God, what was it about this woman that knocked his world a little off-center? It was more than him finding her hot. She was kick-ass and didn't seem to be afraid or intimidated by anyone or anything. Seeing her like this—a little bit vulnerable and raw, made him want her even more than he knew he did.

"And if I do this," he said, dipping his head to gently kiss her lips, "does that distract you too?" he asked.

"Yes," she whispered. A man cleared his throat outside of her broken door and she groaned. "Hey Joel," Melody said without even turning to see who was standing outside her kitchen door. "Come on in and mind the broken glass. We started to clean it up but—"

"Let me guess, you got a bit distracted?" he asked. Shit, Joel had heard them and that was the last thing Axel wanted. He didn't want to cause Melody any trouble.

"Um, I'm going to slip on some pants, be right back," Axel said. He reluctantly released Melody, surprised that she didn't seem to want to let him go. She probably just didn't want him to leave her alone with her boss, but he couldn't answer questions in his boxers. She was at least right about that part. The rest of it though, she was completely wrong about. Melody wanted him; she was just having a hard time admitting it out loud. As soon as they were finished answering questions, he was going to have some fun getting her to admit her feelings, then he was going to take her someplace safe because whoever was coming for her, knew just where to find her.

MELODY

Joel waited for Axel to disappear from her kitchen and walk upstairs to his room, shutting the door a bit louder than she had anticipated. Melody jumped at the sharp crack of the door being slammed and she wondered if she had somehow pissed Axel off. That would be a mistake because she had a feeling that he'd be the only person left on her side after Joel and his guys left her home.

"Want to tell me what the fuck is going on here, Melody?" Joel asked.

"No," she sassed. Telling Joel that her number one suspect in the case, just days ago, was now wheedling his way into her home and her heart, would be a huge mistake. Plus, as her boss, it was none of his business, but they were once more than that to each other and her sense of obligation was going to win out—that was just who she was.

"I like him," she sighed.

"So I gathered," Joel spat. "Have you lost your mind?"

"What—no," she insisted. "I'm of perfectly sound mind," she said.

"He's a suspect in the murder case that you're working," Joel reminded.

"Was," she corrected. "He was the suspect, but the video footage and his alibi cleared him."

"How did you even get involved with him?" Joel asked.

"I'm not really involved with him," she admitted. Joel shot her a look as though he didn't believe a word she was saying, and she couldn't blame him. He had walked in on a pretty "involved" moment if she was being honest.

"Melody, do we have to play games, or are you just going to answer my questions?" Joel asked.

"Fine," she spat. "I went to the bar where he hangs out—the one where he said he was during the murders. I had to check out his alibis and well, I found him there. We had a beer and then the next day when everything panned out and I could tell him that he was cleared from the case, I found him at the bar again."

"He seems to hang out at the bar an awful lot. You sure he's good company?" Joel asked.

"Yes," she said, sounding a bit more defensive than she wanted to. "He's a good guy and he's a part of the biker's club that meets at the bar. They all seem like pretty decent guys. Axel and his partner, Hart, own a detective agency together and they offered to help me with a few leads. They even talked to Ginger's former roommate—the one she lived with before she moved in with Axel."

"Did she have any new leads?" Joel asked. Melody was happy that he seemed to be getting off of the topic of her and Axel and asking about the case now.

"Yes," Melody said, "she told them that Ginger used to date a guy from their club—Savage Hell. She recognized the patch on the back of Axel's jacket and said that the guy was seeing Ginger just before she hooked up with Axel."

"So, there could have been another guy in the picture while Ginger was with Axel?" Joel asked.

"Possibly," Melody said. "But don't you think Axel would have caught on?"

"Not necessarily," Joel said. "I mean, this little arrangement was going on right under my nose and I had no clue."

"We aren't together anymore, Joel," she whispered, looking out the side door to make sure that the two uniformed officers that Joel had brought with him weren't listening in on their conversation. Not many people knew about her and Joel, and she planned on keeping things that way.

"I know that, Melody," he breathed. "I just thought that we shared things and well, you never mentioned Axel."

"I don't think that rubbing your nose in my dating life is the way to go, do you?" she asked.

"I appreciate that," he said. "Still doesn't make me feel any better though, seeing you with him the way you were."

"It wasn't what you think," Melody insisted.

Joel smirked down at her. "It's exactly what I think," he said. "I have eyes, Melody. I saw the way that he was looking at you and you looked at him the same way. You can deny it all you want, but I walked in on something happening between the two of you."

Axel cleared his throat from the hallway, and she groaned again. "What is it about the two of you walking in on private conversations?" she asked.

"It's what makes us damn good cops," Joel said. "We pick up on things that others miss." He nodded to Axel and started to survey the kitchen. "I'm guessing that's the brick?" he asked.

"Yes," Melody said. "We were sleeping," she said, "um, in separate rooms, and I heard a crash. I ran into Axel's room and got him, and this is what we found. We cleaned up a bit of the glass to make things safer, but that note was attached to the brick."

Joel crossed the kitchen to read the note that sat on the counter, not bothering to pick it up. "So, you're next?" he asked.

"Looks that way," Melody said.

"Shit," Joel growled. "I'm taking you off the case," he said. "We'll put you in protective custody until we can find who's done this."

"No," she shouted. "You can't take me off the case. I'm the lead detective. If you give this case to someone else, it will go dead, and Ginger's murder will never be solved. I have too much invested in this case to be pulled off of it."

"It's too dangerous," Joel said. "And you know better than anyone that I don't have the manpower to give you a full security detail."

"How about if I can provide her security detail? I mean, we're already both invested in finding out who murdered Ginger. I'll keep her safe," Axel promised.

"While you two cavemen are trying to figure out who's going to be my big, bad protector, I'd like to remind you that I'm quite capable of taking care of myself," Melody said. She hated when men found her less capable than she actually was. "I have the same training as the both of you."

"Sorry," Axel said. "But when you have some asshole tossing bricks into your kitchen window, that makes you less capable. You're going to have to constantly look over your shoulder, waiting for this asshole to strike again. What if I'm back there, watching your six for you?" he asked.

"You ex-military?" Joel asked.

"Yes," Axel said. "Army," he breathed.

"I was in the Marines," Joel said. He turned to face Melody and smiled, "I'll approve Axel's agency as extra protection for you," he said. "That way, Axel will get paid and you won't be able to deny the extra security. It will be sanctioned by my office, and you will not go anywhere without him, got it?"

"You're doing this on purpose," she said. "To prove your point." Melody knew that she was right. Joel had made an assessment about her and Axel and now, he was going to prove to her that he was right and enjoy watching her squirm in the process.

"I have no idea what you're talking about," Joel said. "I'll have my officers take your statements. I'm assuming that you'll be moving her to a safer location?" he asked Axel.

"Yep," Axel agreed.

"Now, just a minute," Melody protested.

"Text me the details and stay in touch. In the meantime, I'm going to question Ginger's old roommate myself. Maybe I can get a description and we can match up one of the guys down at your club. He might be a lead to the killer. Hell, he might even be Ginger's killer and we can put this shitshow in our rearview."

"Thanks, man," Axel said. "I'll text you her name and address once I get Melody locked down." She put her hands on her hips and stared Axel down.

"Good luck, man," Joel said. "You're going to need it."

☠︎ ☠︎ ☠︎

Melody told Axel that he had to be kidding when he told her to pack her bags for at least a few weeks. He promptly assured her that he wasn't kidding and that they'd be leaving before sunup. As if she'd be able to leave her home, her job, and her life behind for three weeks.

Axel stayed true to his word when he dragged her suitcases out to his truck and dumped her stuff inside. Then, he did the same with her, dragging her to his truck, under protest, and helping her into the passenger seat of the car. He even buckled her damn seatbelt for her before shutting her door quickly getting into the driver's seat.

"This is ridiculous," she spat as she "I don't need to leave my house to be kept safe," she insisted. "I can take care of myself."

"I know that you can," he said. "I'm fully aware of how capable you are, but I need for you to give me just a little bit of leeway, here," he said. "Just let me do what your boss has hired me to do, honey."

"Don't call me honey," she said. "You're forcing me to do something that I don't want to do. So now, you don't get to call me honey."

He chuckled, "Okay, honey."

"Where are you taking me?" she asked.

"Not too far out of town. We need to be close enough to get back for the case." He pulled out onto the highway and headed out of town. She watched the signs pass by her window as the sun began to peek up over the horizon.

"Where will we stay?" she asked.

"A safe house that Hart has arranged for us," he said. "I like to use my own resources when I have a client," he said.

"So, that's what I am now—a client?" she asked. Just a few hours ago, he held her up against his body, while he made her admit to feelings for him that she wasn't ready to say out loud. Sure, she thought that he was hot. Yes, she wanted him

—what red-blooded woman wouldn't? He looked like a bad boy and was even in a biker's club. God, she wanted him more than she'd ever admit, but he had her giving him more truths than she was ready for.

"No," he whispered. "You know that you're more than that, Melody. Hell, I've already kissed you, honey. I want you, and you being my client isn't going to change that."

"What are we going to do about you wanting me?" she asked.

He laughed, "Don't pretend you don't want me too," he said.

She was done denying him, and ultimately herself. Melody wanted to be done with all that. "I won't deny it," she said. "I want you too. I just didn't let myself admit it because you were my main suspect."

"I get it," Axel said. "But I'd like a chance. When we get to the safe house, I'd like for you to agree to be in my bed." She wasn't sure that was such a good idea. The last thing she needed was to complicate everything between them by sleeping with Axel.

"I'm worried that will mess up our working relationship." Melody fidgeted with her hands, and he reached over to take one into his own.

"Just try," he begged. "We'll never know unless we try," he said. He was right, and she hated that.

"Fine," she agreed. "I'll try."

"Thank you," Axel said, raising her hand to kiss her knuckles. "Was that so hard?"

"Yes," she sassed. "I do have one question."

"Shoot," he said.

"How will we get into town and back out to the safe house every day?" she asked.

"At first, we won't," he said. "We're going to lay low and let Joel ask a few questions. Then, we'll start to come out of hiding slowly. I've got another vehicle set up and ready for us to use, just in case they got the tag number for my truck or your car."

"How long will we be laying low?" she asked. Melody knew that he wasn't going to give her much of a choice in the matter.

"Five days, maybe even a week," he said.

"What the hell are we going to do for a week, locked up in a safe house? The case will go cold by the time you let me back out," she spat.

"I'm not keeping you there, honey. You're free to go whenever you want, but you need to remember that someone has threatened your life. Are you willing to forfeit that to get out of the house for a few hours?"

God, she hated that he was making so much sense. Melody was thinking irrationally, with her emotions, and that never ended well for her. "No," she growled. "I'll play things your way for now, but I have to warn you, I'm not very good at being cooped up."

"I'm a lot like you, but maybe we could use this time to go over the case together, compare notes and all that," he said. She was hoping that Axel would suggest spending their time getting to know each other better. Melody felt as though she knew nothing about the guy, except what she had researched when he was a suspect in her case.

"That sounds like a good plan," she reluctantly agreed.

They drove another thirty minutes and she wondered if they were ever going to get to the safe house. "This is us," Axel said, pulling onto a gravel path that seemed to lead back into the woods.

"Are we camping?" she asked.

He chuckled and shook his head. "No," he said. "I don't go camping if I can help it. I had to do enough roughing it in the Army. You'll see the house in a minute—it's a bit off the beaten path."

As Axel drove around the corner, she saw the little cabin and thought it was the sweetest little house she'd ever seen. "This place is great," she said. "It's downright adorable."

"It's a cabin," he said, looking a bit put off that she had called the cabin "Adorable." "Cabins are manly, not adorable."

"Right," she agreed. "Well, it's downright manly," she corrected.

"You might change your mind about how adorable it is when we get inside. It's pretty rustic," he said.

"Wait—tell me that there is electricity and indoor plumbing," she begged. She wasn't the kind of girl who did well camping. In fact, she avoided it at all costs.

Axel chuckled, "Yeah, we have electricity and plumbing. I've already told you that I'm not a big camper. Come on, let's get in and I'll show you around," he said.

"All right," Melody agreed. She was already exhausted from the little trip across town, and the sun had only just come up.

AXEL

He had only been to the cabin a handful of times with other clients but bringing Melody to this place made him nervous—as if he was showing her around his own home. It was ridiculous, really.

"There is only one bathroom, so we'll have to share," he said. He was trying to work his way up to getting her to agree to share his bedroom with her. She had agreed to try during their drive-up. She even agreed to be in his bed, when he asked, but he didn't want to hold her to that if she had changed her mind.

"This is the spare room," he said, pointing into the room on the right. She peeked her head in and nodded, continuing to follow him down the hallway to the master bedroom. "And this is the master," he said. Melody walked in and dumped her bag onto the bed.

"Do you mind if I grab a shower?" she asked. "I didn't get a chance to take one before we left."

"Sure," he agreed. "While you do that, I'll make us something to eat. It's been a long night." She nodded and he put his bag in the corner of the room, not sure if she'd still be willing to share the master with him. He'd move to the spare room if that was what she wanted.

"Axel," she whispered as he left the room. He turned back and she smiled at him. "Thank you for everything," she said. "I've never really had someone protecting me. It's just a lot to get used to because I'm usually the one doing the protecting."

"I get that," he said. "But it's okay for you to let go and have someone else watching your ass for a while." She nodded and he left the room, wanting to give her a bit of space to decide her next move. After they ate, he was going to press her for an answer as to where he'd be sleeping because he needed to get some shut eye if he was going to be able to keep his promise to her and protect her from whatever was coming for them.

After her shower, Melody joined him in the kitchen, her hair still wet and hanging down her back. God, she looked sexy standing there in just her leggings and t-shirt, with her feet bare, waiting for him to finish up lunch.

"Feel better?" he asked.

"Yep," Melody said. He handed her a plate of food and she thanked him, crossing the kitchen to sit down at the table.

"You seem quiet," she said. "And I don't know you very well, but from what I do, I'm guessing that you have something you want to say but are mulling it over. Why not just spit it out?" she asked. Axel was surprised that she seemed to know him that well. She was right though; he was keeping his question in, and it was killing him not just asking her.

"Do you still want to sleep in my bed?" he asked.

"I thought that was clear when I tossed my stuff into the master bedroom," she said. "Have you changed your mind and that's why you're questioning me?"

"Not at all," Axel said. "I just don't want to push you into something you might not want."

"Well, I've already admitted that I want you, Axel. So, I'd like to give this a shot and see where we land. Truthfully, I'm exhausted right now, and all I want to do is sleep. So, if you're good with me sleeping in your bed today, that works for me."

"I'm tired too," he said. "I feel about ready to drop, so a hot shower and sleep sound good to me."

"Let's finish lunch and I'll do dishes while you shower," she offered.

"Thanks," Axel said. He hated how awkward this whole conversation felt, but he wouldn't move forward with Melody without talking things through first.

Axel got out of the shower and pulled on a pair of sweatpants, opting not to just wear his boxers to bed with her. Melody was unpacking her stuff into one of the two dressers in the room and turned, looking his body over. He loved the way she took him in from head to toe. He could see that she wanted him and not have her just giving him the words meant more to him somehow.

"Hey," he breathed. "Ready for some sleep?"

"I don't know," she whispered. "You might need some more clothes if I'm going to be able to sleep next to you. I had no idea that you worked out," she said.

"You're saying that your intel on me didn't have me going out to the local gym every day?" he asked.

"No," she breathed, her eyes flying to his mid-section. "But judging from your abs, you work out every single day." He ran his hands over his abs, and she let her eyes follow their movement.

"It's just something that I picked up doing while in the Army. I had to stay in top shape and well, exercising helps me to blow off steam, so that's a plus," he said. Melody tossed the last of her things into the top drawer and closed it, walking across the small room to the bed.

"Well, you make me feel like a slug," she grumbled.

"Oh, come on," he said. "You work out, Melody," he said.

"I do when I have time. But with the cutbacks down at the department and having to take on more hours, I just can't seem to find the time to go to the gym. Where do you go?" she asked.

"I have a home gym in my basement. It's why your intel didn't have me going to the gym every day," he said, flashing her his grin. The less time he spent out in public, the less likely it was that he'd be spotted when on a case. He liked his privacy and the anonymity that having a home gym gave him. "You're welcome to become my first member," he teased.

"Are the membership fees steep?" she asked.

"I'm sure that we can work something out," he joked, bobbing his eyebrows at her. Melody's giggle filled the room and it sounded magical. Why was he so entranced by this woman? Just days ago, she was trying to toss his ass into prison and throw away the key. Now, she was sliding into bed with him, and he wanted her more than he did his next breath.

He watched as she got into the bed and wondered if she was always going to wear so many clothes to bed with him. Since their lunch, she had slipped on a sweatshirt and looked about ready to head out for the day, not hop into bed with him for a nap.

"You're wearing an awful lot of clothing," he mumbled.

"I'm cold," she lied, raising her chin as if daring him to call her a liar.

"Sure, honey," he said. "Well, I'm burning up." He pulled his sweats down his body, letting her look him over in just his boxers. He loved the way her breath hitched a little and her chest heaved as though she had just run a marathon.

"What are you doing?" she asked.

"I'm getting comfortable. I usually sleep naked, but we're not there yet. So, I'll keep on my boxers," he said. Melody almost looked disappointed, and he chuckled to himself as he slid into his side of the bed.

Melody pulled the covers up her body, covering herself to her chin, so all that he could see of her was her head. She was ridged and Axel could tell that she was completely out of her comfort zone.

"You all right?" he whispered, closing in on her side of the bed.

"What are you doing?" she whispered.

"You ask me that question a lot," he teased. "I'm getting comfortable, and you don't look very cozy over on your side. Come here, Melody," he ordered. At first, she didn't make a move toward him. But then, he wrapped an arm around her, underneath the bedding, and pulled her against his body. Once she seemed to realize that he wasn't going to give up the fight, she gave into him, even seeming to relax some against his body. Her ass was practically seated on his cock, and he knew that he wouldn't sleep much with her like that, but he was a masochist and liked the way that she wiggled against him. Melody didn't seem to have any idea how she affected him, but she was going to find out—sooner rather than later.

"Night," she said around a yawn, snuggling into his body.

"It's technically day," he whispered into her ear.

"Well, that just sounds weird," she said. Before he even got another word out, she was softly snoring.

"Night, Melody," he whispered tugging her closer. Axel wasn't sure how he was going to sleep with the raging boner that he was sporting, but he needed to get a few hours of shut-eye if he was going to be able to keep her safe—and right now, that was his only goal.

Axel woke up and the room was dark. He checked to see what time it was and rolled away from Melody, instantly regretting doing so. She was warm and the house had gotten cold while they were sleeping. He found his sweatpants and tugged them on. Axel quietly rummaged through his bag and found a sweatshirt, pulling it on over his head. He was going to start a fire to warm up the cabin, and then, he'd check in with Joel and Hart. He had promised both of them to give an update at dinner time and that had passed a few hours ago.

He got the fire going and pulled out a few things he needed to make dinner for the two of them. He was going for something simple and cold cuts seemed to fit the bill. Luckily, Hart had the place stocked for them while they were driving over that morning.

First, he needed to call Joel and make sure that he had things under control on his end. He hoped that Melody's boss might have some good news for them or at least a lead, but it hadn't even been a day since they left town.

"Hello," Joel answered.

"It's Axel," he said. "Calling in for the daily update."

"Shit, Axel," Joel grumbled. "You were supposed to call in about three hours ago. Everything all right?" he asked.

"Yeah—we fell asleep, and I guess we were pretty tired because Melody is still in bed." He decided to leave out the part where she was in his bed. That would just be rubbing salt in her ex's wounds and that wasn't the kind of guy he was.

"Nothing new here," Joel said. "You talk to your partner yet?" he asked.

"No, you were my first call when I woke up. If Hart has any news, I'll call you back. If not, Melody or I will check in tomorrow at dinner time," he promised.

"Don't blow past your check-in time again, or I'll send some of my guys out to make sure that you guys are all right. Got it?" Joel asked.

"Yep," Axel agreed.

"Talk tomorrow," he said.

"Absolutely," Axel said, ending the call. He knew that Melody's old boss was flexing his muscle, showing dominance, but he didn't give a fuck. He was going to play things his way and if Joel didn't like that, well, that was just too fucking bad.

"Hey," Melody said, walking into the kitchen. "It's cold in here," she said, wrapping her arms around her body. Axel pulled her into his arms, sharing some of his body heat.

"I just started a fire, but it's going to take a bit to get warm in here. I called Joel and he's pissed that I was late calling in. I guess we overslept a little."

"Yeah," Melody yawned. "I feel like I could sleep straight through the night, but I'm hungry."

"Me too," he agreed. "I got some sandwich stuff out, does that work?"

"Sure," she said. "I'll make us dinner."

"I appreciate that, honey. I still have to call to check in with Hart. Give me just a minute." She nodded and he found Hart's number in his phone, calling it, putting it on speaker.

"What the fuck happened, Axel?" Hart growled.

"Good to talk to you too, man," Axel said.

"Don't try to charm your way out of this," Hart said. "I'm not one of Savage Hell's barflies. What the hell happened?"

"We fell asleep and just woke up. It was a long damn night." Axel held his breath, waiting for Hart to come back with some kind of asshole comment about him napping with Melody, and he instantly regretted putting the call on speaker. Hart surprised him by not making the comment and he knew that his friend was holding back. When Hart started falling for Shannon, Axel gave him a ton of shit, so it would be only fitting for his friend to do the same back.

"I don't have much of an update for you," Hart admitted. "It's been a slow day, sorry."

"Tomorrow's a new day," Axel said. "Besides, Joel didn't have much success either, if that makes you feel any better."

"It doesn't," Hart mumbled. "But thanks for trying. Try to check in on time tomorrow," he said, ending the call.

"That went better than I thought it would. I expected Hart to give me some shit for falling asleep on the job," Axel said. He left out the part about him not wanting to tell his friend about them ending up in the same bed together.

"Hart seems like a stand-up guy," she said. "I appreciate you both helping out with this mess." She handed him a plate with two sandwiches on it and he nodded his thanks.

"Let's eat and then we can go back to bed," she said. He could tell that she was still tired and there was no way that he'd push her for more yet. If he did, and things didn't work out, he worried that she'd take off on him, and then, he wouldn't be able to keep Melody safe.

MELODY

Melody woke up to the sound of someone rummaging around downstairs and she grabbed her gun from the nightstand. Her feet hit the hardwood floor and she realized that she wasn't at her house. She followed the noise, gun in hand and when she turned the corner into the kitchen, she came face to face with the barrel of a gun.

"What the fuck, Melody," Axel spat. "I thought you were still upstairs sleeping. You're like a fucking ninja. I almost shot you." She looked at the gun he had pointed at her face and smiled.

"Well, I could ask you the same thing," she said. "Plus, I might not have killed you, but you would pee sitting down for the rest of your life." Melody nodded down to her gun that she had pointed at his cock, and he raised his eyebrow at her—something that she found sexy as hell.

"Shooting me there would definitely put a damper on what I've promised to do with you, honey," he said. "How about we just both lower our weapons and you can tell me why you're sneaking around the cabin."

"I couldn't sleep and well, I heard a noise down here and decided to check it out. I didn't even think about it being you. Hell, I've been alone so long, I don't think of someone being in my house, or well, the cabin where I'm being kept under lock and key."

He chuckled, "You aren't being kept under lock and key," he insisted. "I've already told you that you're free to leave whenever you'd like. But you'll put yourself in danger if you do."

"I'm good with you keeping me here, Axel," Melody said. "In fact, I'm kind of getting used to it." She had gotten used to having him around over the past week that they had been locked away together. Every night, he held her, and they slept tangled up together, but that's as far as Axel took things. He'd touched her, held her hand, and even kissed her a few times, but he was moving at a snail's pace, even though she had already given him the green light. It was almost as if he was afraid to take her, and she wondered why.

"Have you changed your mind?" she asked.

"About finding the flashlights that I was looking for?" he asked. "Because we're supposed to have a storm and they will come in handy. The electricity usually goes out when that happens."

"No," she said. "I'm not talking about flashlights. I'm asking you if you've changed your mind about wanting me."

"What? No, of course I haven't changed my mind," he said. "I just don't want to push you. We've only known each other for a few days now, and I don't want to rush you into something you might not be ready for."

"It's been a week, Axel," she almost shouted. "I've known you for over a week now, and I want you to rush me. Hell, I wanted you the first day we got here, but you haven't made a move." She crowded his space and wrapped her arms around his neck. "If you want me, why not make a move, Axel?" she asked.

"I don't know," he admitted. "I'm afraid that I'm going to fuck everything up and that's the last thing I want to do. I like you, Melody, and the more time that I spend with you, the more reasons I find to not make you mine. If I mess this up, you'll walk, and I don't want you out there when we don't know who or what we're dealing with."

"So, you won't take me because you're worried that we won't work out and I'll just leave?" she asked. He nodded and she went up on her tiptoes to gently kiss his lips.

"What if I promise to stick around?" she asked. "We're both adults here, Axel, and we both know what we're getting into, right?" she asked.

He nodded, "Sure."

"All right then," she whispered. "Make me yours, Axel, please," she said.

"You're absolutely sure?" he asked. She was done waiting

for him to make a move. She was a take-charge kind of woman and sitting around waiting for a man wasn't her style.

"Yes," she said, reaching down to cup his cock with her hand. "I'm sure." She liked the way that Axel's breath hitched, and she couldn't help her giggle.

"You have no idea what you've started," Axel warned. He lifted her up against his body and tossed her over his shoulder as though she didn't weigh anything.

"Put me down," she squealed. "Axel, you can't do this."

"I can," he said, starting up the stairs to her bedroom, "and, I am doing this. You started this, honey." He gave her ass a swat and she squirmed at how good that felt. She had never been one for spanking, but having his hand warm her ass felt right—it felt good.

"I know," she breathed.

"Tell me now if you've changed your mind," he ordered. She wasn't about to change her mind about Axel ending up in her bed. She wanted that with him.

"I haven't," she insisted. "I won't change my mind, Axel."

"Thank fuck," he growled, tossing her onto the bed. She squealed and giggled, loving this playful side of him. Axel usually acted the big, bad biker persona he was trying to portray, but underneath, he was sweet, gentle, and even playful.

"I like seeing this side of you," she said.

"Well, that's good because I plan on showing you all of my sides," he teased. Axel unzipped his jeans and let them hit the floor, leaving him completely naked for her to look over. Melody sat up and looked him over thoroughly.

"You're so big," she breathed. "And is that a piercing?" she asked.

He looked down at his cock and back up at her, smiling, and nodding. "It is," he admitted.

"I didn't have you pegged as a guy who'd have his dick pierced," she said as if accusing him of wrongdoing.

"I was a dumb kid who accepted a dare. A couple of my MC buddies and I were drunk off our asses and they dared me to get my cock pierced. Hurt like a bitch, but after it healed up, I thought, why not?" he said. She thought it was just about the sexiest thing she had ever seen and all she wanted to do was run her fingers over the piercing. Hell, she wanted to lick it, but they would hopefully get to that.

"Can I touch it?" she whispered.

"Yes," he moaned. "I want you to touch me, Melody," he said. She reached out and stroked her hand over his cock and he thrust into her hand as if demanding more. He hissed out his breath and she wondered what else she could do to make him lose some more of his tightly held control.

"Can I taste you?" she asked. He growled and nodded, and she knew that he wasn't in control anymore—she was. She was taking everything he was willing to give, and that thought was a heady one for her.

Melody leaned down and let her tongue lick over the head of his cock, playing with the stud in the end. "Stop teasing me," he hissed. She giggled and sucked him into her mouth, letting her tongue swirl around his shaft. God, he was big and so very demanding, she worried that she had gotten in over her head as he nudged the back of her throat. But then, he pulled back out, allowing her to breathe, and she let her guard down a bit. He knew what she needed and was willing to give it to her, all she had to do was give him a little trust. The only problem was, she wasn't sure if she could trust him or not. Letting her guard down might not be the best way to handle Axel, but what choice did she have? Wanting him wasn't an option—she did. Now, all she had to do was find a balance between wanting and trusting him, and that was going to be a tough road to walk.

He pulled free from her mouth, and she mewled out her protest, causing him to chuckle. "It's not funny," she slurred. She sounded as though she had been drinking, but she was sure that the only drug she had taken that night was Axel. He was intoxicating and Melody wanted more.

"I know, honey," he said. "I wasn't laughing at you. It's just so damn cute when you make those little sounds. I want to be in you when I come though. You good with that?" he asked.

"I am," she quickly agreed. "I'm on the pill."

"I can still suit up if you want me to," he offered.

"No," she breathed. "I want you just the way you are, Axel." Maybe she was playing the fool, but Melody didn't care. She wanted to feel him skin on skin.

Axel quickly stripped her out of her nightshirt and hissed

out his breath when he realized that she wasn't wearing anything underneath. "You're hot as fuck, honey."

"Thank you," Melody breathed. "You are too." She grabbed his cock and he moaned, thrusting into her hand again. "I need you inside of me," she hissed. He didn't seem to need to be told twice. He slid into her body, causing them both to moan at just how good it felt. It had been a damn long time for her since she had been with a man. Axel's stud hit a spot inside of her that she had forgotten existed and she wasn't sure if she wanted to laugh or cry at just how good it felt.

"Right there," she shouted. "Don't stop, Axel." He smiled down at her as he pumped in and out of her body, setting a furious pace. She wasn't sure if she'd be able to last very much longer, and honestly, she didn't want to. She wanted to find her release, to fly, to soar even, and Axel was giving her the wings to do it.

She found her release and he didn't take long to follow her over, spilling his seed deep inside of her, claiming her. That's what it felt like too—Axel was claiming her body, mind, and soul and there was nothing that she wanted to do about it.

AXEL

Axel's cell rang and he sat up in bed, looking over to make sure that the noise hadn't woken Melody. She was still lightly snoring next to him, and he grabbed his phone and headed downstairs to the kitchen, to let her sleep longer. He hadn't been easy with her last night, keeping her up most of the night, and letting her sleep was the least he could do.

"Hello," he growled into the phone.

"Morning, sunshine," Hart said.

"Why the hell are you calling me so early?" Axel asked.

"It's almost eight," Hart countered. "You never sleep this late—you feeling all right?"

"I feel fine," Axel barked. "Why the hell are you calling me, Hart?"

"To give you an update. The video footage came back,

and Joel made some leeway with Ginger's old roommate. I thought you might want an update."

"Yeah," Axel said. "Let's hear it."

"Joel was able to convince Ginger's old roommate to join him at Savage Hell. I have to admit, he really seemed to fit in at the club," Hart said.

"Focus, man," Axel warned.

"Right," Hart mumbled. "He brought her down to the club and she was able to point out the guy that Ginger was with before she moved in with you. Savage showed her those damn pictures that he takes of new members. You know, the ones that look like mug shots?"

"Who is it?" Axel asked.

"Spider," Hart said, "and he's the guy on the video, dragging Ginger's body to the corner of that alley. Looks like Spider has moved to the top of our suspect list."

"That's great," Axel said. "Not about Spider, but about maybe solving this case sooner than later." He wanted to get back to his life, but he needed to come up with a way to keep Melody in his life because letting her go now wasn't an option.

"You seem to be in a hurry, man," Hart accused.

"Not really. I just want my life back," he admitted.

"I get that," Hart said.

"Do we know why Spider killed her?" Axel asked.

"Allegedly killed her," Hart corrected.

"Sure," Axel agreed. "Do we have any answers? Were you and Joel able to bring him in to question him?"

"No," Hart breathed. "There was a hiccup."

"What kind of hiccup?" Axel asked.

"Joel went to Spider's apartment with an arrest warrant, and he wasn't there. The guy seems to have disappeared from the face of the earth—no one can find him." Axel softly cursed to himself. The last thing they needed was to have their murder suspect go missing. They might never catch up with him, and that would suck.

"I'm guessing that returning to our normal lives won't happen any time soon," Axel grumbled.

"Looks that way," Hart said. "But we're doing everything that we can to find him. When we do, you'll be the first to know. For now, you two need to stay put and lay low."

"I know the routine," Axel said. "You just find Spider so we can get our answers, and I'll worry about Melody and me."

"Will do," Hart agreed. "Talk soon." He ended the call and tried to decide if he was going to make a giant pot of coffee or go back to bed and cuddle with Melody. The decision was made for him when she appeared in the kitchen doorway, wiping sleep from her eyes, and looking sexy as fuck.

"Morning," he breathed.

"Good morning," she whispered. "Coffee?" she asked. Melody's cell phone rang, and she sighed. "You work on the coffee, and I'll see who that is."

"Deal," Axel agreed. She disappeared back to the bedroom to answer her phone and moments later, was back with the call on speaker.

"It's Joel and he has news," she said.

"I've already gotten an update from Hart," he admitted. She shot him a look and he shrugged. "You were sleeping," he defended.

"Go ahead with the update," she told Joel.

"Well, we got the video footage and Ginger's old roommate cooperated. Spider was the guy that Ginger was two-timing Axel with and well, he was the one in the video dragging her body into the alley. We just have to link him to the actual murder, and I think we have our man."

"That's great Joel," she said. "Did you pick him up?"

"That's where things get hairy," Joel admitted. "I went by his place and he's not there. I've also done some digging on the guy and he's ex-military. He was in the Marines, dishonorably discharged for bad behavior. Apparently, the guy has a laundry list of fights on his rap sheet. The last one that got him kicked out of the Marines was a doozy. He put a guy in the hospital, and they weren't sure that he was going to make it. This guy should be in jail, but somehow, he's evaded doing any time. There's also a warrant for his arrest in Texas and Colorado, but no one has been able to bring him in."

"Shit," Axel grumbled. "He's been under our noses this whole time and we just accepted him. You tell Savage yet?" he asked Joel.

"Yeah," Joel said. "That guy is a beast. I went over to your club with Heart, and we told him together. He's pretty pissed off. If I was in Spider's shoes, I'd be more worried about

Savage catching up with me, than I would be about the law coming after me."

"No doubt," Axel agreed. "What do we do now? What happens if we can't find this guy? With a military background, he might never be found, and then what happens to Melody and me?" he asked.

"We'll figure that out as we go," Joel assured. "Right now, I need for you two to stay put while I try to find this guy."

"Or," Melody started. Axel and Joel both groaned at the same time, knowing that she was going to have a plan that neither of them would like. "Or," she repeated a bit louder, "we use Axel and me as bait and we can flush him out."

"No fucking way," Axel said. "I don't mind being used as bait, but there is no fucking way that you'll be involved."

"How do we know that this guy isn't coming for you and not me?" Melody said. "I mean, he knows you and has for a year now. I'm just the detective working the case."

"And the one he'd go after if he felt threatened," Joel insisted. "Just stay put and don't go marking yourselves as bait just yet. Give me a shot at bringing him in first."

"Fine," Melody reluctantly agreed. "But I won't stay locked up here forever. I'll go crazy, Joel," she insisted.

"Good luck Axel," Joel teased. "She's a handful when she feels cornered. You two stay safe."

"Thanks, man," Axel said, just before Melody ended the call. "I like him," he said.

"Great—my current boyfriend likes my ex. That makes me feel so much better."

He smiled at her, and she looked at him as though he lost his mind. Melody had no idea that she had just called him her "boyfriend," but Axel had to admit, he liked the sound of it.

"What?" she asked.

"You called me your boyfriend," he said, still smiling at her.

"Is that okay?" she asked. "I mean, what else should I call you?"

"Works for me," he agreed. "I just didn't quite know where we stood after last night, but now, I do. So, that would make you my girlfriend," he said, pulling her into his arms.

"I guess it does," she agreed. "Wow, I didn't have you pegged as the mushy, romantic type," she teased. "Big, bad biker likes it when I call him my boyfriend—who knew?"

"Don't go around telling people that," Axel insisted. "I have a reputation." She giggled as he kissed her. "How about that coffee?" he asked.

"Yes, please," she agreed. "I think we should take it back to bed and after we're done drinking our coffee, we can pick up where we left off last night."

"I like the way you think," Axel agreed. He grabbed his mug of coffee and followed her back to the master bedroom. If he had to be locked away in a safe house, he couldn't think of a better way to pass the time than with Melody naked and panting out his name underneath his body. Yeah—this sure beat his other assignments, and now, he had a girlfriend to boot.

Axel's Grind

They spent almost a month locked away in the cabin and while the sex was fantastic, he could see Melody's spirit waning being locked up day after day. He called Hart to let him know that they were going to town to pick up some groceries. Axel promised her a trip out of the house and Melody seemed to perk up some. He couldn't go back on his word now—it would crush her.

"It's just not safe," Hart chided. "I can order the things you need and have them discreetly delivered. Spider is still out there."

"And for all we know, he could already have eyes on us. He might be just sitting and waiting for us to leave the house, to make his move. When he does, Melody and I will be ready. I think that what you and Joel are forgetting is that we're not helpless victims in all of this—we're highly trained and can hold our own."

"Right, but Spider is a bit crazy and that makes him dangerous. He's got mental issues that make him a threat, and you two need to remember that," Hart insisted.

"Got it," Axel growled. "Spider is dangerous—anything else?" he spat.

"You know what? Do what you want, man. Your mood is shitty and I'm not going to be on the receiving end of your attitude," Hart said.

"You try being locked away for almost a month and see how you're attitude fairs. I'm done with this shit. I'm ready to get my life back and if that means that Melody and I put ourselves in danger, we're okay with that." Axel could feel her eyes on him. She had been there for the whole phone call and every time he looked at her, she was nodding her agreement, giving him her silent support.

"I get it," Hart said. He didn't get it. How could he? The longest time his partner had spent on assignment, away from home, was a couple of weeks. "But just give us a little bit more time, and I'm sure we'll find Spider."

"No," Melody said. "We're done hiding away. I won't come home, but we need some groceries, and we're going to go get some fucking groceries."

"All right," Hart breathed. "You two just be careful, please."

"We will be," Axel agreed. "I'll text you when we're back here safely."

"I'd appreciate that. I'll let you know if we have any updates," Hart offered. It had been a month of him and Joel taking turns calling to give them daily updates and Axel was sure that he'd lose his mind he had to hear that they had no news again for another day. He ended the call and pulled Melody into his arms.

"Sorry that I interrupted," she said. "I just couldn't take any more. I need to get out of this place," she admitted.

"Me too," he agreed. "Let's get dressed and I'll take you to breakfast. I know this great little restaurant. Then, we can run our errands and maybe even pick up some dinner for later. What do you say?" he asked.

"I say, yes!" she almost shouted at him, causing him to laugh. He kissed her and God, he wanted to tell her that he had fallen in love with her, but were they there yet? Every time he tried to broach the subject with Melody, she'd change it. Honestly, he could see that she felt the same way that he did, but she was just too afraid to say it. Axel just hoped that they'd get to that point some time along their journey.

"Ready to get moving?" she asked as if picking up on what he was thinking. She was once again distracting him from saying how he felt about her, and he'd let her win—this time.

"At some point, we're going to have to talk about what's happening between us, Melody," he whispered.

"Don't be such a girl, Axel. We don't have to discuss our feelings. This isn't a high school sleepover. Let's just get dressed and get out of here."

"Fine," he grumbled. "Be ready in ten." She nodded and ran off to their bedroom and he wondered if he hadn't just made a huge mistake letting her put him off again.

***

Axel spent most of breakfast sulking and he could tell that Melody picked up on his sour mood. "Well, this is fun," she mumbled under her breath. "I hope that you're not going to act like a five-year-old all day."

"I'm not acting like a child," he challenged.

"Well, you're being awful moody and quiet," she accused.

"I'm being quiet to keep an eye on everything around us. Spider could be watching us right now, and I'd like to see him coming if that's what he has planned."

"All right, well, while you keep an eye out, I'm running across the street to that cute little boutique. I need a few new things because I didn't pack enough for a month. Maybe you should go over there, to that store," she said, pointing out the diner window, "and pick up some new things too."

"This is what I get for bringing you to a diner in a strip mall," he grumbled.

"Yep," she agreed. "We can meet back at the truck in thirty minutes. Does that give you enough time?" she asked.

"To buy some extra socks and underwear?" he asked. "I think I can be done in five. But you can have thirty minutes," he amended when she glared at him. "I'll meet you at the truck then."

She got up and kissed his cheek on her way out. "Thanks, Axel," she said. He watched as she walked out of the diner and made her way across the street. Melody was keeping an eye on her surroundings, but he breathed a sigh of relief when she made it into the store without any trouble.

Axel paid their bill on the way out of the diner and quickly made his way into the store, doing a quick check to make sure that he hadn't been followed.

"Can I help you find something?" a woman who worked there asked.

"No," he barked. "I can find what I need. Thanks," he added to soften his grumble. He quickly made his way around the store and found everything that he needed, even a few new outfits, which he was sure Melody would be happy about. They were doing laundry every other day and it was getting old. He just needed to try on the jeans and then, he'd make it back in time to meet her at the truck. He paid for his things and walked back across the parking lot to where his truck was parked, finding no sign of Melody.

He pulled his cell from his pocket and quickly called her, wanting to know that she was all right. "Hello," she answered. "I still have eight minutes before I'm late." He could hear the amusement in her voice.

"All right, well, I just wanted to check on you," he said. "I'm here waiting—take your time."

"Thank you," she said. "I will." He chuckled to himself and hung up his cell, putting it back into his pocket, and tossed his bags into the back seat of his truck.

"Well, isn't that sweet?" a man's voice said from behind him. "You've gone and found yourself another woman. And so soon after Ginger's murder." He turned to find Spider standing behind him, holding a gun to his side. "Don't do anything stupid," Spider warned.

"Wouldn't dream of it," Axel mumbled. "What do you want, Spider?" he asked.

"I think it's about time that you and I had a chat—brother to brother," he said. Axel hated that Spider was considered his brother, but in the MC world, they were linked as brothers, and he'd try to remember that and not strangle the guy with his bare hands for all of the trouble he had caused him.

"Where's your sweet little girlfriend hiding?" he asked.

"Don't know," Axel lied.

"Mmm," Spider hummed. "We can play things that way if you'd like. You'll do for now, until she and I can catch up. Let's go," Spider insisted. He shoved the barrel of his gun into Axel's back, and he knew that he was out of options. He had to go with Spider to keep Melody safe. It was the only way because if they stuck around talking, Melody would make her way over to the truck and Spider would take her too—or worse. He walked over to Spider's truck and got into the passenger seat, as he was directed.

"Slide over to the driver's seat. You're going to drive so that I can keep my eyes on you," Spider ordered. Shit, if he was a passenger, he'd have the chance of using Spider's driving as a distraction to get the gun away from him. Spider was proving smarter than Axel expected him to be and that might end up being a problem.

He slid across the seat and quickly looked over to the store where Melody was shopping. He saw her watching the two of them out of the front window and he could almost see the promise in her eyes that she was going to find him, no matter what. His girl was smart—not rushing out to cause a scene in the parking lot. It would probably end up getting both of them killed and there were a large number of innocent shoppers that would be put in danger. Melody wouldn't allow that to happen.

He didn't maintain eye contact with her, not wanting to give away her location to Spider. "Let's go," Spider said, pulling his door shut. "I want to get to where we're going before nightfall."

"Where are you taking me?" Axel asked.

"You'll see soon enough," Spider promised. "I wouldn't want to give away the surprise."

"You're an ass," Axel accused.

"I'll let that one slide," Spider said. "After all, you've just been kidnapped, so you're allowed to be grumpy." Telling Spider that he was an ass again wasn't the way to go. It seemed to only make him happy as if Axel was playing right into his hands. He just needed to keep a cool head and make it to their destination. Axel knew that Melody would have his six and would call in a rescue squad. Hopefully, he'd still be alive to see her again.

MELODY

Melody was just about to walk out of that store and over to Axel's truck when she saw another guy standing there with him. At first, she thought that maybe he was a friend of Axel's, the way that the two seemed to be chatting, but she got a closer look at the guy and realized that it was Spider.

She wanted to run out there and demand that Spider let them both go, but she also knew that doing so would put the both of them, along with everyone in the area, in danger. So, she did the hardest thing she'd ever done—stood by and watched the man she was in love with being taken away. It was her only option, but that didn't mean that she felt good about it.

Melody grabbed her cell phone from her pocket and

called Joel, letting him know what was happening and he told her to stay put, but she wasn't about to let Spider drive off with Axel and not follow him. She told her boss that she was going to follow Spider's truck in Axel's, keeping a safe distance, and he protested. When she told Joel that he had no choice in the matter, he sighed into the phone and told her to be careful and wait for backup to show. She made no promise, but she also wasn't a fool. Running into save Axel without a team behind her would be signing both of their death certificates. She knew that much, and it wasn't something she was willing to do.

She followed as closely as possible but still stayed back enough to not be spotted. They drove for what felt like an eternity and when Spider's truck pulled into a warehouse that looked to be abandoned. She drove by as if on her way to someplace else and called the location into Joel. He promised her that his team would be there in about thirty minutes, but she wasn't sure if Axel had thirty minutes to wait for them to find him. She promised to stand down, but that wasn't a promise that she was about to keep. Melody parked around the block and headed for the side entrance of the warehouse. There was no way that she wouldn't have Axel's back and the only way she could do that now was to be in that warehouse with him. She'd stand back out of sight until her backup got there, but if Axel needed her, she wouldn't hesitate to act.

She snuck into the side entrance, thankful that the

ancient building didn't seem to have an alarm system in place. Melody listened for any sound from the floor below and when she heard Axel's voice, she felt a sigh of relief. He was still alive and that gave her hope. For now, she'd have to be content in standing back in the shadows and waiting things out for now and pray that Joel would be able to get his team into position sooner than later.

☠☠☠

Melody hid in the shadows, hoping that her backup would show any time now. Joel had ordered her to stay put and not go into the building, but she couldn't just leave Axel alone with Spider. His MC buddy was crazy and from the way that he was shouting at Axel, she was sure that waiting for backup wasn't going to happen. She held her gun to her side and stayed in the dark corner, hoping like hell that Joel was truly five minutes away because she was sure that Axel didn't have much more time than that.

"You ruined everything," Spider shouted. He had his gun pointed at Axel's mid-section and a shot fired at that range would end up killing him. She couldn't let that happen—Melody couldn't lose him, not now. "Ginger was mine and then, you showed up in her life and took her away from me. I begged her to come back to me, but you were so controlling, she was too afraid to leave you."

Axel barked out his laugh, garnering him another back-hand to the mouth. "Shut the fuck up," Spider growled. "You don't get to fucking laugh at me Axel—not anymore. I bet that's what you and Ginger used to do every night, right? Did you get off laughing at the poor sap who was sitting at his home, heartbroken, begging her to come back?"

"Man, I didn't even know that you existed," Axel taunted. She wanted to tell him to shut the fuck up, to save himself a beating, but he was trying to keep Spider talking, and that might just buy them some more time. "Ginger never told me that she was with you. Hell, she never talked about you at all, Spider," he said. That earned him another punch to the mouth and Melody winced when Axel spat out blood.

"That's not true," Spider shouted. "She loved me, and you confused her. You kept her from me," he yelled.

"I didn't keep Ginger from anyone. You knew her—there would be no controlling that woman. If she wanted you, she would have gone back to you, man," Axel said. She held her breath waiting for Spider to punch him again, but he didn't.

"She wanted to come back to me," Spider said. "That's what she told me that night that she died. Ginger said that you were keeping her from me and that she was sorry."

"But you killed her anyway?" Axel asked. Spider hadn't confessed to the murder yet, but Melody knew that was what he was angling for.

"I had to," Spider whispered. "Ginger left me no choice. She promised me that she was going to come home with me, that she wanted to be with me. She told me that she just had to grab a few more things from your apartment and then, we'd be together. But she never showed up at my place that night. So, I went out looking for her. Lucky for me, I had her new address already from watching her, so I tried there first. When I asked her why she didn't come over, she told me that it was over and that she had lied, but I knew the truth," he said.

"What was the truth, Spider?" Axel asked.

"That you got to her when she was picking up her stuff. You convinced her to leave me again. You were trying to steal her from me again, and I couldn't let that happen, so, I stabbed her."

"In the heart," Axel finished for him.

"I thought that was fitting since she had ripped my heart out by doing what you told her to do. Now, it's your turn to be punished," Spider said. Shit—they needed more time and Spider seemed ready to get the show on the road.

"Why come after Melody?" Axel asked. He was smart, coming up with more questions. Their only hope was that Spider wouldn't grow tired of Axel's little game and silence him forever before help could arrive.

"Because she stopped looking at you as a suspect," Spider said. "At first, I planned on leaving town, but then, she took you into custody and I thought that they would find a way to pin the murder on you. Savage went and got that cocky asshole, Razor, involved and you walked. When the detective found the video footage of me dragging Ginger's body into that alley, and dumping her behind the dumpster, I had to do something. I thought that if your new girlfriend disappeared, she'd stop snooping around the case and the trail would eventually go cold."

"But it didn't," Axel said. "You just bought us time to do more research and have our team look into you. We got too close, didn't we, Spider?"

"Yes," Spider agreed. "And as soon as I'm finished here with you, I'm going to find that bitch detective and kill her too." Melody's cell phone buzzed in her pocket, and she said a little prayer that Spider wouldn't be able to hear it. If she had to guess, Joel was letting her know that he was at the abandoned warehouse, and that was just what she needed to hear.

"You won't have to come find me, Spider," Melody said, stepping free from the shadows.

Axel groaned and she shot him a look. "What are you doing here, honey?" he asked.

"Who'd save your ass if I didn't show up?" she sassed

She looked Spider over as he gripped the gun tighter. "Well, this just frees my night," he said. "After I kill Axel, I'll take care of you too, and be home in time for dinner."

She waved her gun around, letting him know that his plan wasn't going to go exactly as he hoped. "You kill Axel and I'll have you on the ground before you even take your next breath," she warned.

"Can we come up with a plan where I'm not dying?" Axel grumbled.

"You're not going to die, Axel," Melody promised.

Spider laughed and she looked him over. He was clearly not in his right mind, so she'd need to proceed with caution.

"How about you put the gun down and we can talk things out," Melody offered.

"No," Spider said.

She shrugged. "All right. Just remember that I gave you an out, Spider."

He smirked at her, "You might be able to kill me after I shoot Axel, but you'll have to live without him for the rest of your life," he said. That thought terrified her, but she didn't waver. "That's not what I want though," Spider said. He pointed his gun at her. "I want Axel to know what it feels like to lose everything. I want him to have to live without you. I guess the question is—who's the faster shot."

She could see her team in the shadows and now, it was her turn to smirk at him. "Actually," she breathed, "the question is which one of my team members has you in their scope. You see, while you were confessing to Ginger's murder, my team had the time that they needed to get here and move into place. You're completely surrounded, Spider," she said as her guys stepped free from the shadows.

"Put the gun down and this can all end peacefully," Joel said. "I can promise you that you won't even get off a shot, Spider. It's over." Joel took a step toward Spider, his gun pointed at his chest, and she could tell that Spider was actually weighing his options.

"Don't do it, Spider," Melody said. "No one else has to die."

Spider turned to Axel, pointing his gun at him again, and she held her breath. "He should be the one you're pointing your guns at," Spider spat. "Axel is the one who killed Ginger. She died because of him and his controlling her. This is all his fault." Axel looked like he was trying to hold it all together, but she could see the fear in his dark eyes. Spider wasn't in his right mind and one simple squeeze of the trigger could end everything that they had been building.

"I'll take full responsibility," Axel lied.

"Just put the gun down and we can work this out," Joel assured. They were both lying. As soon as Spider dropped the gun, they'd have him in handcuffs.

"What guarantee do I have that you'll arrest him and not me?" Spider asked.

"You have my guarantee," Savage said, stepping in from the side entrance. "You will be treated fairly." Hart and Savage stood on one side of the room, staring down Spider, looking as though they wanted to tear him apart.

"Brothers don't do this to each other," Savage added. "As your Prez, I'm telling you to stand down, Spider," he ordered. Spider was former military and Melody just hoped that his notions of duty would win out and he'd follow Savage's orders.

Spider hung his head, looking Axel over one last time as if trying to decide what to do. "We'll get you the help that you need, man," Axel promised. "You're not alone in any of this."

"How do I know that I can trust you?" Spider asked.

"We're brothers," Axel said. "You'll just have to trust. I promise to tell the court that you need help when I testify. I'll ask for leniency and ask the judge to put you in a facility that will be able to help you, Spider. I'm ex-military too and I know how hard is to find your way again once you come home."

"I was never even given a chance," he said. "I got back, and they just discarded me so easily."

"I know man," Savage said. "We'll help you figure it out, just drop your gun." Spider nodded and Melody felt as though she was willing him to do as they guys were asking. She just needed for this all to be over.

Spider squatted down slowly to put his gun on the floor and stood back up, his hands in the air. "I'm going to hold you to your promise, Axel," Spider said as Joel's team swooped in to cuff him and read him his rights.

"Understood," Axel agreed. "You have my word." Melody rushed to his side and cut the duct tape that bound his hands and feet to the chair. He stood and pulled her into his arms, and she didn't fight to hide her sob.

"I'm so relieved that you're okay," she cried.

"Me too," he agreed. "I thought for sure that I was a goner there, but I knew that you'd find a way to get to me and bring in your team. Thank you, honey," he said.

"Always," Melody whispered.

"Sorry to break this up, but I'm going to need for Axel to come into the station to give his statement," Joel said.

"We'll follow you," Axel assured. "You mind driving, honey? I'm still a little shook up."

"Absolutely," she agreed. She had so much that she wanted to say—the most important was that she loved him, but that would wait until they were alone. Then, Melody would spill her guts to him and let the pieces fall where they might.

AXEL

They spent the rest of the day down at the station, giving their statements to Joel. Axel still felt a bit shaken up every time he thought about what might have happened if Melody hadn't followed him and Spider to that warehouse. He would have never seen her again, but most of all, he would have never been able to finally tell her that he was in love with her. Dying with that kind of regret couldn't be good and he wouldn't take that chance again. Today, after this whole mess was done, he was going to finally tell Melody that he loved her. This time, he wouldn't let her change the subject or push him off. He was going to tell her that he wanted forever with her and if she didn't like it, well, he'd deal with that later.

"What's going to happen to Spider?" Axel asked Joel.

"That depends on the judge," Joel said. "But I'm betting

that if you two show up with a few of your guys from Savage Hell, you'll be able to convince the judge to get him the help that he needs. They don't have enough resources for Vets, but I'm hoping that you can help him come up with something."

"He doesn't belong in prison. He needs a hospital and doctors who can help him," Axel agreed. "I know that he killed Ginger, but he was delusional when he did it. As a Vet myself, I know the horrors that we have to face down daily. Some of us just handle things better than others."

"I'll do my best to get Spider where he needs to be," Joel agreed. "What's next for you two?" he asked, smiling between the two of them.

"Well, I'd like to go home and take a nice long bath," Melody said.

"I've had your back door fixed and have been keeping an eye on your place for you. I think you're good to return home," Joel said. "How about you?" he asked Axel. That was a damn good question. He didn't want to go back to his empty apartment. He wanted to go home with Melody. Hell, he didn't want to have to go anywhere without her, but that would be up to her and a conversation that he'd want to have in private.

He shrugged, "I'll figure something out," he said.

"Well, I'll be seeing you soon," Joel said. "I'm looking into joining Savage Hell. You think I'll make a good Royal Bastard?" he asked.

"That's great," Axel said. "And yeah—you'd be perfect for our club. I can sponsor you if you need one," he offered.

"Thanks, Axel," Joel said. "That means a lot." He walked them out to the parking lot and told Melody not to come in tomorrow. Joel said that he'd see her Monday morning, bright and early, and her face lit up. Axel could tell that she was looking forward to getting back to work and back to her life, but would that life include him?

Joel left them standing in the parking lot, next to Axel's truck. "Will you give me a ride home?" she asked.

"Of course," he agreed.

Melody smiled and took his hand into her own. "Will you stay with me?" she asked.

"Are you asking me to?" he questioned.

"Yes," she breathed.

"For how long?" he asked.

"Forever," she answered. "I'm in love with you, Axel. I want you to stay with me forever." He started to talk, and she covered her hand over his lips. "Seeing you bound to that chair with a gun pointed to your head, was eye-opening for me. I've been avoiding my feelings for you, believing that this would all be over once Spider was taken into custody, but then something clicked inside of me. I don't want to avoid my feelings anymore, Axel. I want you to know how much you mean to me."

He pulled her hand from his mouth, gently kissing her fingers. "It's about time," he mumbled. "I love you too,

Melody. I'd like to stay with you—forever," he quickly added, causing her to giggle through her tears.

"Really?" she asked.

"Really," he said. "I've been trying to tell you how I feel about you for weeks now, but every time I did, you shot me down. Waiting you out was exhausting, but I'm so glad that I did. I love you, honey."

She held out her hand to him and he took it. "Then, let's go home," she said. "And start our forever."

"Now, that sounds like a damn good plan," he growled. Axel had been watching his brothers at Savage Hell drop like flies, falling for the women who knocked them on their asses, and now, he finally knew just how they felt. He'd completely fallen for his woman, and he wouldn't have it any other way.

The End

I hope you enjoyed Axel and Melody's story. Now, buckle up for your inside sneak peek at Razor's Edge (Savage Hell Book 6).

RAZOR

Razor walked into the courtroom to meet his newest client. Savage had called to wake him in the middle of the night, to go downtown to help him out with a problem. He was supposed to meet with some woman who went by the name Firefly. He knew that her name was Penny Quinn, he just had no idea that Savage's little problem downtown would be Razor's walking wet dream, or that she was resourceful enough to get herself out on bail. He just hoped that she was going to be showing up at the arraignment, or his whole case was fucked. Hell, it was already fucked since he didn't even get the chance to talk to her yet about the case. She could be a total nut job, and he'd be fucked having to represent her anyway. He'd do it too because he owed Savage his fucking life.

He walked to the front of the courtroom and found a

pretty redhead sitting up before the judge's bench. He'd seen her around Savage Hell but never talked to her before.

"Firefly," he said, sitting down next to her. "Savage sent me."

"Of course, he did," she mumbled. "I've already told him that I'm good. I can handle things on my own."

He looked her over and nodded, "Of course, you can, but I'm a lawyer and I'd be happy to help you with your case. You know since I'm already here."

"That's so sweet of you," the redhead said. "But I think I'm good." She smiled at him, quietly watching as if her dismissing him would have him moving his ass out of the chair next to her. What the hell was he supposed to do now? He promised Savage that he'd help her, but if she refused his help, there was nothing that he could do. He'd just have to tell Savage that he tried and hope that the big guy believed him.

"Suit yourself," he grumbled. He got up from the table and walked to the row of chairs just behind where she sat, sitting down directly behind her.

"What do you think you're doing?" she whispered back over her shoulder.

"I'm not leaving until I have a report to give to Savage. He will want to know what happened to you and I plan on being able to tell him," Razor said.

"Fucking bikers and your stupid notions of duty," she mumbled. "I told you that I've got this," she insisted.

"And I told you that I'm not leaving here until I can tell

Savage what happened," he spat. The bailiff walked into the courtroom and told everyone to stand for the judge and Razor was just happy to get this shit show started. All he wanted to do was report back to Savage and go back to his bed. He hadn't had a good night's sleep for days and he was finally hoping to catch up on some much needed shut eye.

"Be seated," the judge said. "Is Miss Quinn present?" she asked.

"I am, your honor," Firefly said, standing from her seat.

"Where is your council, Miss Quinn?" the judge asked.

"I'm representing myself, your honor. I'm a third-year law student and feel capable of handling this," Firefly said. Well, that was news to Razor. He'd seen her around the bar, but never really asked too many questions about her. It was a good thing too because, from the sounds of it, she was much too young for him. He had just celebrated his forty-second birthday and well, she had to be about twenty-five. Razor was almost old enough to be her father.

"Well, you are in a bit of trouble, Miss Quinn," the judge chided. "You stole about thirty dollars' worth of groceries, and then when you were caught, you tried to punch the officer. Is that correct? How do you plead to the charges that I've just read to you?"

"Not guilty, with explanation, your honor," Firefly said.

"Let's hear it," the judge said.

"I've used my savings to pay for my last semester and had just enough left over to pay for my rent. I've recently lost my job and I was hungry. I only took enough to get by. I'm looking for another job right now, but no one is hiring since all of the college kids got back to town." Hearing that broke Razor's damn heart. He could tell that she was having the same effect on the judge. He'd been dead broke when he graduated from law school. He even held off on taking the bar until he could save up a bit of money. He didn't want to hope for a job as quickly as he was able to land one in the legal community.

"I see," the judge said.

"If I may, your honor," she said, holding up her hand as if she was in grade school.

"Yes," the judge said.

"I didn't attack an officer. I attacked a guard who worked security for the supermarket. I would never attack an officer of the law. The only reason I slapped the guard was because when he frisked me, he grabbed my ass. Legally, he's lucky I'm not suing him or the grocery store chain." She looked over to the table where the owner of the store stared straight ahead as if he hadn't even heard what she had just said.

"Is there any proof of this?" the judge asked.

Firefly smiled and nodded. "I recorded the whole thing on my phone, your honor," she said.

"Ah, technology," the judge breathed. "Let's see the footage," she ordered. The judge held out her hand for Firefly to approach and she did, removing her cell phone from her pocket and handing it up to her.

"It's the only saved video on my phone," she said. The judge found the one she spoke of and watched it, volume up at full, and the courtroom could hear the whole ugly scene as it played out. Razor could even guess when the guard had grabbed her ass in the video, hearing Firefly's gasp and then the sharp slap she administered, probably to the guy's face.

"Wow," the judge said, handing her back her cell phone. "Honestly, I would have slapped him too. Is this the kind of behavior that you approve of from your employees?" she asked the store owner.

"No," he said. "I had no idea that was happening when I told the head of my security to search her. But she stole from me," he insisted.

"I understand that," the judge said. "Please take your seat, Miss Quinn." Firefly walked back to the table and looked back at him just before taking her seat. Razor wondered what the look she shot him was about. Firefly sat down and faced the judge again.

"The way I see it, you have a choice to make," the judge spoke to the store manager and Razor had a good idea how she might handle the situation. "You can press charges for the items that Miss Quinn took but didn't get away with. In which case, I'd advise her to press charges against your store and your employee for sexual harassment. Or you can drop the charges and hope that Miss Quinn is also in a forgiving mood and doesn't press charges against your store and your employee. What's it going to be?" she asked.

The store owner sighed and turned to his lawyer. The two men had a hushed conversation that seemed to go on for minutes, not just seconds, and then he stood with his lawyer.

"I'd like to drop the charges in exchange for Miss Quinn signing a statement that she won't press charges against my store," he said.

The judge looked back over to her, and Firefly seemed unsure. "Take it," Razor whispered from behind her. It wasn't the best deal, but it would do to get her out of trouble that could get her kicked out of law school or even keep her from taking the bar. This would keep Firefly's future safe.

"I'll take the deal, your honor," she agreed. "Thank you." The judge nodded, banging her gavel on the giant mahogany desk that she sat behind.

"Dismissed," she said. "Miss Quinn, I'd like to see you in my chambers," the judge said.

"Yes, your honor," Firefly breathed. She turned to look back at Razor, flashing him her sexy smile. "Guess I didn't need you after all," she sassed. She was a feisty one—he liked that attribute in a woman. No—she was a girl and much too young for him to be so attracted to.

"It's not over yet, honey," he breathed, standing from his seat. "You still have to go back to chambers and that is usually not a good thing. You do know that she's not inviting you back for tea, right?" he asked.

The smile vanished from her face, and he almost felt bad for what he had just said to her—almost. "What do you think she wants?" Firefly asked.

He shrugged, "No clue. You want me to wait around?" he asked.

"No," she stubbornly whispered. "I've taken things this

far. I can go the distance." He pulled his business card from his jacket pocket and handed it to her. "The next time you need a little help, call me. I don't mind helping out an up-and-coming young lawyer. You shouldn't have to go without food just to be able to pay your tuition, but I've been there Firefly. You're not alone." Razor turned to leave the courtroom before he gave in to desire and asked her to go out to dinner with him. That wouldn't be a good idea for either of them and probably one she wouldn't entertain anyway. Right now, all he wanted to do was report back to Savage and have a few beers with his buddies. Then, he'd find a warm, willing woman to take back to his place to help him forget all about the sexy redhead with the sad eyes.

FIREFLY

FIREFLY WAS SCARED OUT OF HER MIND AS SHE WALKED BACK down the narrow hallway that led back to the judge's chambers. The last thing she needed was a mark on her record before she even got done with law school. She knew better than to steal the food, but she was hungry and wasn't thinking straight. She was angry that her money had run out and that her father had told her that she was on her own. Hell, that shouldn't have come as such a surprise since she had been on her own for most of her life after her mother died.

She filed into the judge's chamber as the court bailiff held the door open for her. "Thank you," she said back over her shoulder to him.

"Yes, ma'am," he said. The bailiff shut the door behind

her, and she looked around the office. It was very understated, quite like the judge, and sparse in furnishings.

"Miss Quinn," the judge said, entering the room from the side door. She had changed out of her dark robes and Firefly was surprised at how much smaller she looked in her street clothes. The woman was even wearing her sneakers with her business suit and Firefly wanted to giggle at her attire but refrained when the judge pointed to a chair.

"Have a seat," she directed. Firefly did as asked. "I'm sure that you're wondering why I've asked you to come back to my chambers."

"Just a bit," Firefly lied. She was shocked by the invitation and very curious. But her mother used to tell her that curiosity killed the cat, and well, she loved cats.

"I'd like to offer you an internship," the judge said.

"But—" Firefly started.

The judge held up her hand as if stopping her from speaking. "Please, just hear me out." Firefly nodded and she continued. "I admire the way that you held your own in my courtroom. I'd like to offer you a paid internship with my office. It won't be easy—especially with your coursework for the last year of classes, but I think that you'll be fine. Not all of us are lucky enough to receive scholarships, grants, or even have parents who are willing to pay our tuition. I was a lot like you while I worked my way through law school, and I know what it's like to be at the end of your rope. I want to ensure that you graduate, and I have a feeling that you might need a little extra help to do so. Will you take my job offer?" the judge asked.

Firefly didn't even have to think about it. This was an opportunity that she couldn't pass up. "Yes," she almost shouted. The judge laughed and stood.

"Good," she said. "I'd like for you to start tomorrow," she insisted. "You haven't asked what the job entails or pays."

"Doesn't matter," Firefly insisted.

"I think you'll be pleased to know that it is a paid position, but you will also receive a partial scholarship from this office that will pay for the rest of your schooling, book, room, and board."

"That's too much," Firefly insisted.

"Not at all," the judge said. "As I've said, I've been in your shoes."

"Thank you, your honor," Firefly whispered, standing to shake the judge's hand. "For everything."

"See you tomorrow morning," the judge said.

"Yes," Firefly said. "You will." She left the office and walked back down the hallway to the courtrooms. As soon as she turned the corner, she ran right into the big lawyer/biker that she had seen around Savage Hell. It was her guilty pleasure, hanging out at that bar. God, she loved bikers, but she hadn't found one that she wanted to hang out with on a regular basis.

She had been with a few of the bikers—that was how she got her nickname Firefly. She loved her name and used it daily. When people asked her name, she'd tell them that it was Firefly, not Penny. She hated her birth name, and Firefly seemed to fit her better. The guys down at Savage Hell seemed to think so too, telling her that her fiery red hair helped them to come up with her name.

"I thought I told you that I was good," she said to the big guy. If she remembered correctly, his name was Razor. He was a little older than the guys she hung out with normally, but she had noticed him around the club.

"I told you that I wanted to be able to report back to Savage. He was the one who sent me down here to help you. Does he know that you don't need help?" Razor asked.

"No clue," Firefly said. She had met Savage years ago when she was just a kid. He was friends with her mother before she died and after she was gone, Savage took Firefly under his wing. Her father hated that she spent time at the bar, after she turned twenty-one, and maybe that was partially why she did it.

"Listen, I appreciate you sticking around, but I'm going to be fine. I was just offered a paid internship with the judge's office, and I took it. I won't be trying to shoplift food anymore and I'm pretty sure that you won't be getting any phone calls from Savage about me again."

"That's fantastic," he breathed. "Well, not the part about never hearing from you again. But the part about your internship here is great. You must have made quite the impression of the judge if she offered you a position like that."

She shrugged, "I guess."

"I'll let you go," he said. "I'm sure you have better things to do than to stand around talking all night. I remember how challenging law school was, even if it was eons ago."

"I doubt it was that long ago," she said. "Thanks for your help, Razor," she said. He smiled at her, and she wondered if that had to do with the fact that she remembered his name. "See you around Savage Hell."

Razor nodded and started for the door and the next words were out of her mouth before she could decide if she should even say them or not. "Want to grab a beer with me now—you know, at the club?" she asked. God, she sounded like a bumbling idiot.

He paused in the doorway, hesitantly looking back at her. "I'm not sure that is a good idea, Firefly," he said. Hearing him say her name the way that he did made her feel a little giddy. "I'm a hell of a lot older than you."

She smiled back at him. "I really never let age factor into who I like to hang out with, Razor," she said. "It's just a beer—nothing more."

"Just a beer?" Razor asked.

"Yep," she agreed. "How about it?"

She felt as though she was holding her breath waiting for him to answer her, and when he finally nodded, she blew out her breath. "Just a beer," he agreed.

Firefly followed him out of the courthouse and when he walked her to her car and helped her in, she wondered if all older men were so chivalrous.

"I'll meet you over at Savage Hell," he breathed, dipping

his head into her car. "Drive carefully." He shut her door and Firefly felt herself swoon—literally swoon and she shook her head at herself in her rearview mirror.

"Get yourself together," she mumbled to her reflection. "It's just a beer."

Razor's Edge (Savage Hell Book 6) coming April 12, 2022!! Universal Link->
https://books2read.com/u/m0lepY

Don't miss the other books in the Savage Hell series! These titles are available NOW!

RoadKill-> https://books2read.com/u/bWPeRM
REPOssession->https://books2read.com/u/bMXDa5
Dirty Ryder->https://books2read.com/u/3RnyxR
Hart's Desire-> https://books2read.com/u/bpzJ9k

Also, don't miss K.L.'s latest Royal Bastard release! The Royal Bastards is the series that started it all and led to the spinoff of Savage Hell!!! Patched for Christmas is out NOW!!

PATCH

Patch worked her way out of the brush, trying to find the tree line. She knew that once she did, she'd find the guys waiting for her, but leaving Hawk behind was tearing her apart. She knew that she couldn't help him, not now. The bullet had sliced through his stomach, probably hitting more vital organs than she'd ever like to admit, and when he told her to go—to just leave him there, Patch told him the truth. She loved him and had for a long time now. Letting him die in the forest all alone wasn't her choice, but if he wanted her to go and leave him there, then he could just hear her say the words that she had longed to tell him for months now.

Patch was hoping that would change things; that her words would convince him to let her stay with him until the end, but she knew Hawk well enough to know he wouldn't allow that. He wouldn't want her to sit by his side and watch him die. He was about to give her back those same beautiful words when gunfire rained around them. He pleaded with her, demanded that she leave him and go find the others. Patch knew that was the last gift she could give him besides her heart. That also belonged to Hawk now and always would. She bent to gently kiss his lips and took off for the tree line, not looking back. She couldn't look back because if she had, she would have turned around and demanded that Hawk get up and walk out of there with her. She wanted to laugh at how ridiculous that thought was, but all she seemed capable of doing was crying. She swiped at the hot tears that spilled down her face and tried to find the clearing. That was where the helicopter would be waiting to take them home—not that it would ever feel like that again. Not without Hawk.

"Patch," Ratchet called to her, waving a flare over his head, signaling her as to where they were. She ran from the forest and into the field where her team was waiting.

"Where's Hawk?" Mason asked.

"He—he didn't make it," Patch sobbed. "They shot him, and he told me to leave him. I couldn't patch him up—he was too far gone and when they started firing at us, he told me to go. I just left him there," she shouted over the roar of the rotors starting up.

"We have to go," Ratchet said.

"We need to get him out of that forest," she insisted. How had their mission gone so wrong? They were sent to retrieve a scientist that the FBI wanted. It was supposed to be an in-and-out mission. Their intel told them that the place was sparsely guarded, and they were good to go in to retrieve Dr. Simmons, but their source was incorrect. The bunker that they had the scientist in was guarded like Fort Knox. Their team was lucky to get the doctor out of there and safely to the helicopter. Ratchet and Mason had radioed her and Hawk to get their asses to the clearing when all hell broke loose.

She and Hawk were watching the team's six. They were the last line of defense and when the team got out, she could usually breathe a little easier, but not this mission. She and Hawk were practically surrounded by men who were pretty pissed off that they had taken Dr. Simmons. They were running to the tree line and Patch was sure that they were home free when she saw the light coming from the clearing. She turned back to tell Hawk that they were almost to the clearing when he was hit. Patch watched as he grabbed his belly and fell to the ground. It was like watching her whole world collapse in front of her.

"We can't," Ratchet said. "You know that I'd do anything to save Hawk, but we can't go back into that forest, Patch. He wouldn't want us to risk ourselves. They probably have him already and there will be nothing that we can do to get him back. He's gone, Patch," Ratchet croaked. She knew how the big guy felt about Hawk—they were more than work partners, they were brothers. Patch knew that if Hawk could be saved, Ratchet would find a way to do it, but he was right, Hawk was gone and there would be nothing that they could do to get him back now.

"Let's go," she breathed, taking Mason's hand as he helped to hoist her onto the copter. They loaded up and she held her breath as they lifted off, remembering how Hawk had given her shit about being so afraid of those damn birds. She hated being in them and he knew it. Give her a plane any day of the week, but Patch would prefer to steer clear of helicopters; not that there was much choice for missions like these.

She looked back to the forest, knowing that Hawk was down there somewhere. Patch couldn't think about what might have happened to him if they got their hands on him. Was he already gone? That was the question that kept playing through her mind, but she refused to let herself answer it. She knew that answer—he was gone. Patch had lost him and there was nothing she could do to change that.

HAWK

NELSON HAWKING WATCHED HER THROUGH HER LITTLE townhouse window and wondered if he'd ever get up the nerve to knock on her door. It had been almost a year and not going to her and telling Patch that not only had he survived, but that the government had put him back together better than ever, wasn't allowed. He had been given a new identity, a new life, and told to never return to his old one. That was proving impossible for him though because all he wanted to do, day after day, was find Patch and tell her that he loved her too.

She had given him those sweet words before she left him in the forest. He had been shot in the gut, the bullet slicing through his liver, and he was dying. Before she left, she whispered the three little words that he had wanted to hear from her for so long. He just never thought that in a million years, she'd tell him that she loved him. They were colleagues, and working so closely together, feelings would have only gotten in the way. They both knew that and falling for each other wasn't part of the plan. But he had to admit, he had fallen for her too. He wanted Patch and acting on those feelings would only end up getting them and their team killed. So, he pushed his desires for her down, way down deep, and went on with his duties working for the FBI.

Watching Patch walk away from him was the most painful thing he'd ever had to do. He never got to tell her that he loved her and that was something that he hoped to one day rectify, but he worried that doing that would only end up getting them both killed and that wasn't a chance that he was willing to take.

He watched as she put the final ornaments on her Christmas tree that stood in her two front windows. He had only been to her place a few times and he knew how warm and cozy it was on the inside. Hawk loved her townhome—it felt so much like her and seeing her in her place now only brought back the crushing memories of how his life used to be.

Hawk used to have friends, a place in this world, a job he loved, and her—he had Patch if only as a co-worker and friend, he still looked forward to seeing her beautiful face every day. She'd smile at him, and his world would light up. Patch would give him crap about something and he felt like all was right with the universe. Yeah—he was in love with her and not telling Patch was eating a hole straight through his gut.

She stood back and put her hands on her hips as if inspecting her tree and smiled. He couldn't help but smile at the way she gave the spruce a nod of approval. He loved seeing her like this—almost happy. It had been a long time since he'd seen her smile after she thought that he was gone. He never thought he'd see her happy again, but maybe that had to do with the holiday season. Wasn't everyone happy at Christmas?

He sighed and shoved his hands into his pockets. It was cold in Alabama for the first time all season and that made him long for home—or what home had become for him. He was being hidden away up in Michigan and he knew that sooner or later, they were going to call him to come back. He had made up an excuse that he needed to clean up a few of his past mistakes before he fully gave up his life and joined the elite secret group of mercenaries that the government had asked him to be a part of. It was something his time in the military had trained him for, and his new body, specially designed with enhancements to make him stronger, faster, and well—just plain better than he was, had him believing that he could actually do the job that they were asking him to do. Hawk just needed to find a way to let go of his past in Huntsville—to let go of Patch, to do that.

He told himself that all he needed was to see her. He needed to make sure that she was all right without him. He had made a few trips back, after his many surgeries, to see her. He had kept his distance, not wanting to break his promise that he'd stay in the shadows. The government had told him that no one from his past could know that he had survived the gunshot wound and that included the woman that he loved. But it didn't mean that he couldn't check on her. Every time he was in the area, he'd stop by her townhome and stalk her from afar, just like today. But something about today was different—more final. He knew that once he accepted this assignment, he'd never be able to come back to Huntsville again. He'd never be able to watch Patch from across the street, keeping a safe distance to check on her. Hawk would never be able to tell her that he loved her and that just felt wrong. He knew that giving Patch those three little words wouldn't change things for either of them, but he felt like he had to do it, or he'd regret missing his chance for the rest of his life.

"Fuck," he breathed to himself. He was going to break all of the fucking rules and there wasn't anything stopping him. No voice of reason, no government official telling him to get his ass out of there—nothing would stop him from crossing the street and knocking on her door. Nothing except for himself, because he knew that while giving her the words might make him feel better, it would only end up tearing Patch apart and he couldn't do that to her again. It was better if she just believed that he was dead. That way, she might be able to find a way to get on with her life—without him.

"Merry Christmas, Patch," he whispered. Hawk backed into the shadows of the alley. That was where he existed now

—in the shadows. He was on his own and that was the way it had to be, no matter how in love with Patch he was.

Patched for Christmas (A Royal Bastard Christmas Novella) Universal Link-> https://books2read.com/u/bWGQrM

And one more Royal Bastard before you go! Dizzy's Desire (Royal Bastards MC: Huntsville Chapter Book 6), coming soon from K.L. Ramsey!

MASON

Mason Zane was damaged goods—he knew it better than anyone else. But he had this foolish pipe dream of finding a woman and settling down—kids, dog, white picket fence, the whole nine yards. The problem was, he never felt worthy of any of that shit, and meeting the perfect little blond who worked at his favorite corner diner, had him thinking about all of those crazy dreams again.

She was supposed to be his assignment. Her father had hired him to keep an eye on the girl and now, he had to go and let his dick do the thinking for him—which usually didn't end well for him. He wanted the pretty little blond, that wasn't the problem. The issue was that her father was his new boss and from what he understood, the sexy little waitress was in trouble, and she just didn't know it yet.

Brandon Jean told him his woeful story of how he had to

Axel's Grind

walk away from his wife and three small girls when he first started with the FBI. He was supposed to be undercover for just a few months, but then, things went south with his assignment, and he ended up having to take off for a while in order to keep his wife and girls safe.

When Brandon returned home, he wasn't welcomed back with open arms. In fact, he found that his loving wife had moved on with some other guy and had forgotten all about him. He left with his tail between his legs, not even bothering to ask to see his daughters. Brandon told Mason that they were all better off without him. His wife told his daughters that he was missing and probably dead in a gutter somewhere, and that worked for him. In their line of work, it was easier to have loved ones believe the worst about them than put them in danger. If Brandon had reentered their lives, that was what he would have done—put them all at risk, so he decided to walk away.

Now, Brandon was the new head of internal affairs at the Bureau and Mason's new boss. He was being hunted and the men who were trying to find him learned that he once had a family—three daughters and a wife. They were the type of men who'd stop at nothing to get what they wanted, and they wanted to find Brandon Jean. They'd use all of their resources to do so, including the three now grown women who used to call him Dad.

Mason didn't even think twice about taking the job for Brandon. As his new boss, Brandon could have ordered him to do it, but he didn't have to. Mason agreed to the mission as soon as Brandon told him his story. It could have been Mason's story, and that hit a little too close to home.

For years, Mason had toyed with the idea of settling down and having a family, but for that to happen, he'd need to find a woman. None of the barflies at his new MC really appealed to him and he knew that finding that woman to be his forever was going to be harder than finding a needle in a haystack. But then, he walked into that diner to get a closer look at pretty little Dizzy Jean, and he knew right then that he was a goner. She was his walking wet dream and completely hands-off, according to his new boss. Brandon all but threatened to tear Mason's arms off if he so much as thought about touching his daughter. And, thinking about touching her was just about all he could do lately.

He went to that fucking diner just about every day that he knew Dizzy was working, always asking to sit in her booth or at one of her tables. He knew that sooner or later, she'd catch on to him and figure out that he was basically stalking her, but he just didn't care. He didn't care if Brandon found out that he wanted his daughter. Hell, he didn't care about anything except possibly having his chance with her. Mason was trying to get up the courage to finally ask her out, but first, he'd have to make sure that she was safe.

He'd spent the better part of two months watching her from afar, before venturing into that little diner. Dizzy lived in a shithole apartment above the diner with no security measures in place at all. The thought of someone being able to walk into her apartment and take her, terrified him. That was the first clue that he was starting to develop feelings for Dizzy. He had let himself get too close to her and when he stepped foot into that diner, he broke all the damn rules. He blew them completely out of the fucking water, and he didn't give a shit. Rules weren't going to land him a date with the pretty blond, and that was exactly what he wanted—a date with her. It would be his chance to show her that not all guys were assholes because judging from the guys she chose to hang out with—they were all assholes. Dizzy didn't seem to pick the best men to go out with and when they tried to get her to let them go with her up to her apartment, Mason was sitting in the parking lot of the diner, watching, and waiting for his chance to tear the guy apart if he took things too far.

Little Dizzy seemed more capable than he gave her credit for. Not one of those fuckers ever made it up to her apartment with her. She politely smiled and nodded, pushing at the asshole's chest, and shaking her head at him, until he seemed to pick up what she was putting down. Mason wondered if he ever got his chance with her if Dizzy would politely turn him down too. It was one of the reasons why he never got up the nerve to actually ask her out. Hell, he had barely said two words to her and that wasn't his usual MO. He wasn't shy, by any stretch of the imagination, but around Dizzy he felt completely out of sorts—tongue-tied even. He was sick of running out of that diner like a coward every time Dizzy so much as looked at him and smiled. Today would be the day that he'd find the courage to ask her out and let the chips fall where they may. Screw his boss and screw her being his assignment, but first, he was going to run into his new club. He helped out tending bar when Bowie was unavailable, and he wanted to check in to see if they'd need him this week. It was all a part of his master plan to ask Dizzy out. He didn't want any obstacles in his schedule to come up unexpectedly.

He found his new brother-in-law, Ratchet, in the corner of the bar fixing the sound system again. The probies being patched in never seemed to be able to keep the music turned down to a respectable level and this time, they blew the whole fucking system out. If anyone could fix it, Ratchet could. He was like some kind of wizard when it came to fixing shit—it's what he did for the FBI, and he was damn good at his job.

"Hey man," Mason yelled back to him, making sure Ratchet could hear him over the music.

"What's up?" Ratchet yelled back. "Give me just a minute." Ratchet turned off the music and tossed the tool that he was using into the box by his feet. "What are you doing here?" he asked.

"Came in to check out the schedule for the week. I need to see what nights I have free from the bar before I make plans," Mason said, being careful not to tell his old friend who he was making plans with. He and Ratchet went way back—he even saved the guy's life a few times when they were both serving Uncle Sam, but who was counting?

"Plans, huh?" Ratchet asked. "Anyone I know?"

"Nope," Mason answered truthfully.

"If it was someone I knew, would you tell me?" Ratchet asked.

"Nope," Mason said again, causing Ratchet to chuckle. "Where's your work wife?" he asked, referring to his co-partner in crime over at the FBI. Nelson Hawking, or Hawk, as everyone called him, was usually by Ratchet's side. The two seemed inseparable—plus, it was fun to give his new brother-in-law shit whenever he could.

"I'm right behind you, asshole," Hawk growled. "And I'm not the wife in the relationship—he is," Hawk said, pointing at Ratchet.

"Shut the fuck up," Ratchet shouted.

"As amusing as this lover's spat is, I have to get to work. I need to check the bar schedule and head out," Mason said. He headed around the bar and double-checked the schedule, just to be sure that he had read it right. He'd have the whole week off thanks to Bowie being in town this week. He'd have no excuse now for not asking Dizzy out. Not having to work the bar at Savage Hell was a sign from the MC gods themselves—he was supposed to ask her on a date. All he had left was to high tail it over to the diner and ask her out.

"Got to run guys," he shouted over his shoulder on his way out. "Tell Laney I love her, man," he shouted to Ratchet as the door to the bar closed behind him. It was time to face his destiny and hope like hell he wasn't fucking everything up. One way or another, he'd have his answer today. He wanted his chance with Dizzy Jean and the only thing standing in his way was one little word from her—yes.

DIZZY

Dizzy Jean wasn't sure why the sexy ex-army ranger kept coming in day after day, requesting one of her tables, but she had foolishly hoped that it was to see her. It had been a long, dry spell for her between men and God, she wanted the hot, older biker. He was just her type and old enough to feed her "Daddy" fantasies. Yeah—she had issues, but she really didn't give a fuck. It wasn't anyone else's business who she wanted or how messed up she was. That was information she'd just keep to herself and fuck the rest of the people who judged her.

There were a lot of judgmental people in her life too—mostly her family and she learned a long time ago to simply cut them out of her life. It made her so much happier not having them call to tell her how she was fucking up her life every day—especially her mother. That woman had a knack

Axel's Grind

for telling her how she was screwing up. Not once had her mother ever come to her to tell her that she was proud of something that she had done—not even when she was a kid, foolishly seeking her mother's approval at every turn.

Her father, if he could be called that, left her, her two sisters, and her mother when she was just a baby. As the youngest of the family, she didn't really remember her father, besides from the stories that her mom and sisters told about him. From what she was told about him, he wasn't worth wasting her time missing.

The bell over the door dinged and she looked up to find her sexy as sin biker standing there, staring her down. She smiled and nodded to the corner booth and watched him as he made her way over. God, he was even sexier from behind.

Her friend Hilde cleared her throat from behind her. "He's back," she announced.

"Yeah—I have eyes," Dizzy spat. "I can see that he's back." She sounded like a complete bitch, but she hated that Hilde had noticed the way that she watched the big biker, as if she'd have a chance with him. That would make him turning her down hurt even more if she'd ever get the nerve up to ask him out. She had a feeling that he'd have women throwing themselves at him all day long. Dizzy was sure that her doing the same would only land her at the top of his rejection pile.

"What's crawled up your ass?" Hilde asked.

"Nothing," Dizzy breathed. "I just can't figure out why he keeps coming in here asking to sit at my table. It's starting to grate on my last nerve. What the hell does he want from me?" she asked her friend as if she'd have the answer.

"Why not just ask him," Hilde offered.

"I don't even know his name and I'm supposed to ask him why he's basically stalking me? Yeah—I'm sure that will go well," Dizzy grumbled. She grabbed a menu and a roll of silverware, walking away to a chorus of her friend's laughter.

"Hi," she breathed when she got to the corner booth where the sexy biker sat.

"Hey," he returned.

"Um," she squeaked. "The special today is chicken pot pie, but I'd suggest you steer clear. The cook is a little off his game today." The big biker chuckled, and the sound of his gruff baritone made her girl parts tingly. She had almost forgotten what that felt like, to want someone, it had been so long since that last happened for her.

"I'll take the usual," he said, not even bothering to take the menu from her. She put his silverware down on the table and turned to leave. "Thank you, Dizzy," he said, reaching out for her hand, effectively stopping her.

She gasped and turned back to face him. It was the first time that he'd touched her, making her whole arm feel as though it was on fire. "How do you know my name?" she questioned.

He looked her over and gave her his easy smile. "Your name tag," he admitted. She looked down at her uniform and rolled her eyes when she saw the name tag over her left breast.

"Duh," she breathed more to herself than to him. "Well, it hardly seems fair that you know my name, but I don't know yours." That was the first brave thing she had asked him. Usually, their conversations revolved around her telling him the specials and taking his order. She'd check on him more than she had her other customers—to see if he needed a refill or was doing okay. She felt like kicking herself every time he left the diner, and she hadn't worked up the courage to ask him his name—but today, she finally had.

"Name's Mason," he breathed. He was so quiet that she almost had to lean in to hear him and God, the man smelled good.

"It's good to finally meet you, Mason," she said. "I'll run to put your order in," she said, looking down at where his hand still held her arm. "If you don't mind letting me go."

"Oh," he breathed. "Sorry about that, Dizzy," he said. Every time he said her name it made her melt a little. Dizzy wondered what he would sound like whispering her name to her in the dark while buried deep inside of her. She shook her head, trying to rid her mind of her dirty thoughts. She still had four hours left on her shift and thinking about fucking the sexy biker sitting in the corner booth would get her nowhere.

"Not a problem," she squeaked, clearing her throat. "Be right back," she promised. Mason had always ordered a burger, with mashed potatoes—no gravy, a side salad, and a Coke. He seemed to be a creature of habit and she wasn't sure if that was a good or bad thing.

Within minutes, his order was up, and she had to face the biker again. She wasn't sure what to say to him and when she handed him his plate and turned to walk away, he reached for her arm again. "Can you take a break, Dizzy? I'd love some company while I eat."

She wanted to tell him, yes but knew that if she sat down with him, Hilde would give her the stink eye for the rest of the evening. They were unusually busy for a Tuesday. "Can't," she breathed. "We're swamped and there's just the two of us tonight," she said.

"How about a raincheck then?" he asked.

"A raincheck to take a break?" she questioned.

Mason shrugged, "Well, not exactly a break. When are your nights off? I'd love to take you to dinner," he said.

"Like on a date?" she squeaked.

"Um, sure," he agreed. "Like a real date. How about it, Dizzy—will you go out with me?"

"But I don't know you," she protested.

"Well, a date is the perfect setting to get to know someone, right?" he asked. That was a good question—was it a good idea to go out with a perfect stranger? Probably not, but telling him no, wasn't something that she wanted to do.

"All right," she breathed. "I'd like to go to dinner with you, Mason. How about this Saturday?" she asked.

"Saturday works for me," he agreed. She nodded and pulled her arm free from his hand.

"You can pick me up here, at six," she said. At least this way, if things went south, he wouldn't know where she lived

—unless he was smart enough to figure out that her little apartment was just above the diner.

"Sounds like a plan," he agreed. "I'll pick you up here on Saturday at six," he agreed. She smiled and walked away, cursing at herself for taking him up on his offer.

"What did I just do?" she whispered to herself. It was a valid question and one she wouldn't be able to answer. Dizzy had followed her heart instead of her head and that usually ended badly for her. Hopefully, this time would be different, but she doubted it. Matters of the heart usually didn't end well for her, so why should this time be any different?

Dizzy's Desire (Royal Bastards MC: Huntsville Chapter Book 6)—Coming soon from K.L. Ramsey! Universal Link-> https://books2read.com/u/mBwxqp

What's coming up next from K.L. Ramsey? Love at First Fight (A Royal Bastards Valentine's Day Novella) releases on 2/1/22! Here is a sneak peek!

JB

JB Walker slipped into the back of the club, Savage Hell, hoping not to garner too much attention. Of course, having his face beaten black and blue, and his nose busted, made it damn near impossible for him to go unnoticed. His last fight didn't end well for him and that was just the tip of the iceberg. His manager was threatening to drop him, and his sponsors were going to walk unless he got his shit together.

"Fuck man," Bowie spat, handing him a beer from behind the bar. "What the hell happened to you? Your face looks like you've been run over by a truck."

"You guessed it," JB said, giving his club's Vice-Prez a mock salute with his beer before taking a giant swig of it. "I was hit by a truck. Savage around?" he asked.

"Yeah, smartass," Bowie breathed. Bowie was Savage's

husband and always seemed to know their Prez's whereabouts. And if he didn't know where Savage was their wife, Dallas usually did. They were in a happily committed polyamorous relationship and JB wondered how the three of them made it work when he couldn't seem to stick with one woman for more than a night. "He's in the back office."

"Is he in a good mood?" JB asked. He needed to ask his club's Prez a favor, but he would wait if Savage was in a pissy mood.

"Yeah—he just got laid, so I'd say that we're both in pretty damn good moods. Everything all right?" Bowie asked.

"Yeah," JB lied. "I just need a favor."

"Well, I'd say you get your ass back there as fast as you can before one of the other guys ruin his good mood." Bowie handed JB another beer. "Give this to him first—you know, to butter him up." He'd need to do more than just butter Savage up with beer. Once JB told him what he'd gone and foolishly gotten himself involved in, he was pretty sure Savage would need the hard liquor.

"Thanks, man," JB said. Bowie nodded and watched him walk back to Savage's office, down past the kitchen, off the back of the bar. When he got to Savage's door, he turned back to find Bowie give him a nod, as if telling him, "Good luck." He was going to need more than just luck to deal with what was being tossed his way now. He was going to need a freaking miracle.

He knocked on Savage's door, letting the glass of the beer bottle clink against the heavy wooden door. When he heard

Savage growl to, "Come in," he pushed his way into his small office. The guy wasn't big on fanfare, seeming to like things kept simple. He had a desk, a chair, and a small sofa that sat over to the side of the room. On his desk, he had a picture of his growing family with Bowie and Dallas. JB had only been in Savage's office one other time, and he remembered how his Prez gushed about his family. JB wondered if he'd ever have a big brood to brag about to his buddies, but at this rate, that was just a pipe dream.

"What's up, man?" Savage asked, looking up from a pile of papers stacked on his desk.

"I don't want to bother you. If you're busy, I can come back later," JB offered.

"Not at all," Savage said, pushing the papers aside. "I'm just working on the bar order. What can I do for you, JB?" he asked.

He handed Savage the beer that Bowie had sent back for him. "Bowie said to give you this," he said.

"Well, shit," Savage cursed. "I'm guessing that this is going to be something big then if my husband is sending back beer so that you can talk to me." Savage drank down about have of it in one swallow. "Go on," he prompted, pointing to the sofa in the corner.

JB took that as his order to have a seat and telling Savage that he'd rather stand wasn't something that he'd do. "You know how I'm trying to break into the local fight scene?" he asked.

Savage nodded, "I'm assuming that's how you got all that," he said, pointing to JB's face.

"Yeah," he whispered. He gently brushed his hand over his bruised eye and winced. "I had a fight last night. Fucker broke my nose," he grumbled.

"You look like shit, but I didn't want to say anything," Savage said.

"Thanks for that," JB breathed, taking another drink of his beer. "I've lost my last three fights and my manager is threatening to drop me because my sponsors are doing the same. If I lose my sponsors, my manager will walk, and I'll be left with nothing."

"I'm sorry to hear that, man," Savage offered. "But I'm not quite sure how I can help you."

"A few years back, I got involved with a bookie. He was taking bets for me—you know on races, fights, big games—whatever I could lose money on, I bet on it. When I finally decided to pay off my debts and go straight, I told him I was out. I was big money for him, you know?" he asked. Savage nodded as if following along. "So, he told me about a way that I could still help him out and earn a living. He swore it was on the up and up, but I was just a stupid kid for believing him."

"Let me guess," Savage said. "He's the one who got you involved in fighting. Did he hook you up with your manager and everything?"

"Yeah," he said. "I was on a winning streak for so long, he knew better than to bet against me, and I was once again making him a lot of money. But now that I've lost the last three fights, he told me that I'd have to find a way to make it up to him."

"What the fuck?" Savage growled. "You don't owe him shit," he insisted.

"Right," JB said. "But I do. You see, I wasn't joking about being a stupid kid. I signed a contract with my bookie, giving him part of my earnings for his help getting me started. Now, he wants his money back, with interest, or he's going to go after my sister. He said that she'd fetch him a nice payday, and he had a few friends involved in trafficking. If I don't pay him back the sixty-two thousand dollars that I owe him, he'll take Tanya to auction and sell her off to the highest bidder."

"I don't have that kind of money lying around," Savage insisted.

"I'm not here to ask you for a loan, Savage. I plan on fighting again, and I'm going to bet against myself. I'll throw the fight and when I do, I'll get my payday to pay off my bookie. I just need a place that Tanya can lay low. You know—somewhere she can be kept safe until I pay this asshole off. I don't care what he does to me, but I can't let him hurt my little sister."

"That is something I think we can handle. A lot of the guys are coming in tonight and I'm betting we can all put our heads together and find your sister a place to lay low," Savage promised.

"Thanks, man," JB said. "I have until February fourteenth

to pay my bookie, or he'll start looking for my sister. If I know she's safe, I can handle the rest."

"Wow—Valentine's Day is your deadline?" Savage asked.

"Yeah—how's that for a kick in the ass? I have no Valentine and I'm going to have to get the shit beat out of me by one of the top heavyweights in the circuit. Happy fucking Valentine's Day, right?"

"I'd love to tell you that doesn't suck, but it does. Savage Hell will help you keep your sister safe, man. Finding a Valentine and the part about getting the shit beat out of you —well, that's on you, JB," Savage said.

"Gee, thanks, man," JB griped, causing Savage to chuckle. "Seriously, Savage, thank you for the help, man. I don't know what I'd do if something happened to my little sister."

"That's what brothers are for, JB," Savage assured.

CHARLEY

Charley Montgomery walked into the bar her father had told her about. He said that she'd be able to find JB there, but as soon as she walked in to find the place full of bikers, she immediately regretted agreeing to run this errand for her dad. Sure, he was in the hospital and couldn't find JB himself, but the idea of having to deal with handsy bikers at a dive bar wasn't her idea of a good time. All she wanted to do was go home, run herself a hot bath, and soak in it until the water turned cold. But her father's phone call put a halt to that little dream.

How he had gotten himself mixed up in JB's mess was beyond her. Her father had agreed to take on the up and rising boxer at his bookie's recommendation. Who the hell listened to their bookie to make business decisions anyway? Her father, apparently, and at first, it paid off for him.

Her dad would tell her that JB had won his fight and then go on about finding the goose that laid the golden egg. The problem was, his goose had finally been cooked and since he had lost the last three fights, JB was costing him a whole lot of money and almost his life. When JB started costing their mutual bookie friend money, he took off, leaving her father holding the bag, and the guys he had sent after them didn't give a shit who they beat up. When they couldn't find JB, they settled on having to beat her father to within an inch of his life. That was when she got the call from the hospital, telling her that she needed to come down.

It hurt her heart to see her father that way—laying in his hospital bed, helpless, and in so much pain. She wished she could do something to help him and when she made him that offer, he took her up on it. Her dad asked her to find JB and get him to come to the hospital. Her father told her that her life depended on it now, because they'd move on to the next person in line, beating the shit out of every acquaintance JB had until he finally showed his fucking face. He made this mess, and now, she and her father were paying for it. Charley had no choice but to clean up this mess and make sure that the bookie's goons got the right guy to beat the shit out of now because she wasn't about to take a beating for anyone.

A big man with a salt and pepper beard walked up to her and grumbled something about church to her. She had no clue what the guy was talking about. Charley straightened her blazer and pasted on her best smile. "I'm sorry, but I don't understand what you are trying to tell me. Is there someone here who speaks English?" she asked. The big guy looked her over as if she had somehow offended him and then threw back his head and laughed so loudly that it garnered the attention of just about everyone in the bar.

"I speak English, honey," he said. "Name's Savage. I own this bar and am the Prez of this club. Can I help you?" he asked, annunciating every word as if she were hard of hearing or just plain stupid.

"Ah," she breathed. "Lovely to meet you, Savage," she lied holding out her hand to him. "My name is Charley Montgomery. I'm a local CPA in town."

"Numbers cruncher," he mumbled, mostly to himself. "That explains the suit." She looked down her body and back up to him.

"Um, sure," she said. "I've just come from my office. Listen, I'm looking for a man named JB Walker. I was told that I might be able to find him here."

"What do you want with him?" Savage asked, not answering her question.

"Well, it's private business. I'll need to talk to him about it first," she insisted.

"We're all family here, so there is no such thing as private business," Savage said. Some of the other bikers were now surrounding them as if joining in on their conversation. This was just the unwanted attention that she was trying to avoid. JB pushed his way through the crowd and stood next to Savage.

"Sorry about all of this, Charley," he said. "Guys, she's a friend." He turned back to Savage, "You mind if we use your office for a few minutes?" he asked.

"Sure," the big guys said, shrugging as if he didn't care what the two of them did. "You need backup?" he asked.

JB smiled and looked Charley over. "I think I can handle her," he said. Charley had only met JB a handful of times. Usually, when she had to talk to her father, he'd find him with JB. It was like he was the son her father never had and that rubbed her the wrong way. But he seemed like a good guy, besides being a shitty fighter.

She followed him back the Savage's office when he nodded for her to follow him. He shut the door behind them, blocking out the loud music that had resumed in the bar. "What the hell are you doing here, Charley?" JB asked.

"Dad's in the hospital," she said, cutting right to the chase.

"Is he all right?" JB asked.

"No," she said. "He had the shit beat out of him, because your bookie friend, Sal, couldn't find you."

"Shit," he said. "Actually, he was probably looking for Tanya, my little sister."

"Why would Sal be looking for your little sister?" she asked, suddenly feeling very confused.

"Because me losing my last three fights has cost Sal a lot of money. He told me that he was going to take my sister to auction to help him recoup his money."

"Auction?" she asked.

"Yes," he said. "As in, human trafficking. He was going to

sell my twenty-year-old sister to the highest bidder at an auction to get some of the money back that I lost him in the last fight." She looked over his face, noting that some of the bruises around his eyes were starting to disappear. She saw him after the last fight, and he looked like he'd been hit in the face with a baseball bat. His nose was still bandaged, and she guessed that it had been broken during the fight.

"Where is your sister now?" she asked.

He looked her over and smiled. "Safe," he said.

"That's all you're going to give me? My father took a beating for you, and you won't tell me anything other than the fact that your sister is safe?"

"For all I know, you're here to turn me over to Sal's goons. I won't tell you where she is because I can't trust that you won't hand my sister over to save your father," he said.

Charley barked out her laugh. "Wow," she breathed. "Sal's guys are done with my father. They're moving onto me now," she said. "Sal has promised my father that since you're nowhere to be found, I'm next on his list." She turned to walk out of the office. There would be no way that she'd turn over a twenty-one-year-old girl to Sal, no matter how much his goons threatened her, but JB didn't seem to believe that.

"Where are you going?" he asked, putting his hand on her upper arm.

She pulled free from his grasp. "To the hospital to check on my father. Then, I'm going home to have a bath. It's been a damn long day."

"You can't do that," he said. "Sal's men are probably

already waiting for you at both of those places. You can't go anywhere that you usually do, Charley."

"I won't hide away like a coward, JB," she spat. "I have a job to go to and a father to take care of now. If Sal's men want to find me, they will and there's nothing that I can do to stop them." Even though that thought scared the hell out of her, she knew it was true. There would be no stopping them from doing whatever they wanted to do to her. She couldn't go to the police—her father had begged her not to. Some of his business dealings weren't on the up and up and she knew it. Going to the police would only put her father in danger.

"I can stop them," he promised. "Let me help you and Dean out. I won't let them hurt you the way that they did him. Your father means more to me than that. Dean is more than just my manager," he said. "Let me help you, Charley."

She looked back at him and God, he looked so earnestly at her, she wanted to tell him yes. Charley knew that her father would want her to let JB take care of her and keep her safe. If for no one else, she could do that for him.

"Fine," she agreed. "I'll let you help me."

"Thank you for that, honey," JB said, grabbing her arm again. He pulled her along out of the office and back into the bar. "Wait here," he insisted. She watched as JB walked over to Savage to speak to him. He pointed over at her and both men turned to look at her. Charley gave a little wave, not knowing what to do. This was all starting to feel like a giant cluster fuck, and she wondered what she had just agreed to.

JB crossed the barroom and grabbed her hand. "Let's go, Charley," he insisted.

She tried to pull free from him, but he just tightened his grip. "Where are you taking me?" she asked.

"Someplace safe," he promised. She wished that she believed him, but she had no reason to. For all she knew, JB could be delivering her to Sal, to save his sister, and there would be nothing she could do to stop him. He was her only hope now and putting all her hope in one man seemed a foolish game.

Love at First Fight (A Royal Bastards Valentine's Day Novella) Universal Link-> https://books2read.com/u/3kL87R

ABOUT K.L. RAMSEY & BE KELLY

Romance Rebel fighting for
Happily Ever After!

K. L. Ramsey currently resides in West Virginia (Go Mountaineers!). In her spare time, she likes to read romance novels, go to WVU football games and attend book club (aka-drink wine) with girlfriends. K. L. enjoys writing Contemporary Romance, Erotic Romance, and Sexy Ménage! She loves to write strong, capable women and bossy, hot as hell alphas, who fall ass over tea kettle for them. And of course, her stories always have a happy ending. But wait—there's more!

Somewhere along the writing path, K.L. developed a love of ALL things paranormal (but has a special affinity for shifters <YUM!!>)!! She decided to take a chance and create another persona- BE Kelly- to bring you all of her yummy shifters, seers, and everything paranormal (plus a hefty dash of MC!).

K. L. RAMSEY'S SOCIAL MEDIA

Ramsey's Rebels - K.L. Ramsey's Readers Group
https://www.facebook.com/groups/ramseysrebels

KL Ramsey & BE Kelly's ARC Team
https://www.facebook.com/groups/klramseyandbekellyarcteam

KL Ramsey and BE Kelly's Newsletter
https://mailchi.mp/4e73ed1b04b9/authorklramsey/

KL Ramsey and BE Kelly's Website
https://www.klramsey.com

- facebook.com/kl.ramsey.58
- instagram.com/itsprivate2
- bookbub.com/profile/k-l-ramsey
- twitter.com/KLRamsey5

BE KELLY'S SOCIAL MEDIA

BE Kelly's Reader's group
https://www.facebook.com/
groups/kellsangelsreadersgroup/

- facebook.com/be.kelly.564
- instagram.com/bekellyparanormalromanceauthor
- twitter.com/BEKelly9
- bookbub.com/profile/be-kelly

WORKS BY K. L. RAMSEY

The Relinquished Series Box Set

Love Times Infinity

Love's Patient Journey

Love's Design

Love's Promise

Harvest Ridge Series Box Set

Worth the Wait

The Christmas Wedding

Line of Fire

Torn Devotion

Fighting for Justice

Last First Kiss Series Box Set

Theirs to Keep

Theirs to Love

Theirs to Have

Theirs to Take

Second Chance Summer Series

True North

The Wrong Mister Right

Ties That Bind Series

Saving Valentine

Blurred Lines

Dirty Little Secrets

Ties That Bind Box Set

Taken Series

Double Bossed

Double Crossed

Double The Mistletoe

Double Down

Owned

His Secret Submissive

His Reluctant Submissive

His Cougar Submissive

His Nerdy Submissive

Alphas in Uniform

Hellfire

Royal Bastards MC

Savage Heat

Whiskey Tango

Can't Fix Cupid

Ratchet's Revenge

Patched for Christmas

Love at First Fight

Dizzy's Desire

Savage Hell MC Series

Roadkill

REPOssession

Dirty Ryder

Hart's Desire

Axel's Grind

Lone Star Rangers

Don't Mess With Texas

Sweet Adeline

Dash of Regret

Austin's Starlet

Smokey Bandits MC Series

Aces Wild

Queen of Hearts

Full House

King of Clubs

Tirana Brothers (Social Rejects Syndicate

Llir

Altin

Veton

Dirty Desire Series

Torrid

Clean Sweep

Mountain Men Mercenary Series

Eagle Eye

Hacker

Widowmaker

Deadly Sins Syndicate (Mafia Series)

Pride

Envy

Greed

Lust

Wrath- Coming soon!

Sloth- Coming soon!

Gluttony- Coming soon!

Forgiven Series

Confession of a Sinner

Confessions of a Saint

Confessions of a Rebel- Coming soon!

Chasing Serendipity Series

Kismet

Sealed With a Kiss Series

Kissable

Garo Syndicate Trilogy

Edon

Bekim

Rovena- Coming soon!

WORKS BY BE KELLY (K.L.'S ALTER EGO...)

Reckoning MC Seer Series

Reaper

Tank

Raven

Reckoning MC Series Box Set

Perdition MC Shifter Series

Ringer

Rios

Trace

Perdition 3 Book Box Set

Wren's Pack- Coming soon!

Silver Wolf Shifter Series

Daddy Wolf's Little Seer

Daddy Wolf's Little Captive

Daddy Wolf's Little Star

Rogue Enforcers

Juno

Elite Enforcers

A Very Rogue Christmas Novella

One Rogue Turn

Demonic Retribution Series

Sinner- Coming soon!

Graystone Academy Series

Eden's Playground

Violet's Surrender- Coming soon!

Holly's Hope (A Christmas Novella)- Coming soon!

Renegades Shifter Series

Pandora's Promise

Kinsley's Pact

Printed in Great Britain
by Amazon